# Over The
# Moon

# Over The Moon

# JEAN URE

Illustrated by Karen Donnelly

HarperCollins *Children's Books*

For Amy Kampta Maher

First published in Great Britain by HarperCollins *Children's Books* in 2006
HarperCollins *Children's Books* is a division of HarperCollins*Publishers* Ltd,
77-85 Fulham Palace Road, Hammersmith, London W6 8JB

The HarperCollins *Children's Books* website address is
www.harpercollinschildrensbooks.co.uk

5

Text © Jean Ure 2006

Illustrations © Karen Donnelly 2006

The author and illustrator assert the moral right to be
identified as the author and illustrator of this work.

ISBN-10: 0 00 716464 5
ISBN-13: 978 0 00 716464 6

Printed and bound in England by
Clays Ltd, St Ives plc

**Mixed Sources**
Product group from well-managed
forests and other controlled sources
www.fsc.org  Cert no. SW-COC-1806
© 1996 Forest Stewardship Council

FSC is a non-profit international organisation established to promote the
responsible management of the world's forests. Products carrying the FSC
label are independently certified to assure consumers that they come
from forests that are managed to meet the social, economic and
ecological needs of present and future generations.

Find out more about HarperCollins and the environment at
**www.harpercollins.co.uk/green**

Life is so weird: nothing but ups and downs. I can't keep track of it! One 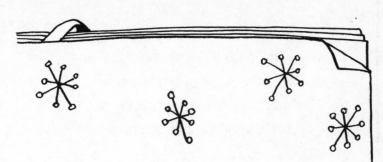 minute it's like whoosh, whiz, sizzle! You're over the moon. And the next, back down to earth with a huge great thump. Down into a pit, full of gloom and despondency and deep dark despair. Which is where I was last night. I just didn't see (I still don't) how Mum could be so mean. So utterly without any sympathy or understanding for my plight. Life

almost didn't seem worth living.
Whereas today – wheeee! All of a
sudden, I'm back over the moon.
Halfway to Venus! Practically out of
sight. I can go to the party after
all!!!

No thanks to Mum. But hooray
for Dad! He is THE BEST. I can
always rely on Dad to stick up for
me.

I wrote that in my diary almost a year ago. I cannot believe that I was so young! Well, I mean, yes, I was twelve. Now I am thirteen, which is admittedly a kind of landmark age when you stop being a mere child and become a proper person. I do think there is quite a big difference between being twelve and being thirteen. All the same... to get so worked up about such utter trivia. Such "small potatoes" as one of my granddads would say. It is truly pathetic.

I was all in a froth, I remember, because I'd been invited to Tanya Hoskins' party, and rumour had it, from people that had been at Juniors with her, that Tanya's parties were something else. I mean, like, really posh. So I'd got this special new gear I was going to wear, a dinky little white outfit, short swirly skirt with matching top, which I'd begged and nagged at Mum to let me buy. It was practically a matter of life and death. I had to look my best! What with Tanya being my number one rival and all. Plus there were going to be *boys*. Even Mum was prepared to admit that boys made a difference, though she muttered her usual mumsy type stuff about twelve being far too young "for that sort of thing". To which Dad, with a wink and a nudge, said, "Oh, yeah? Look who's talking!" It was a bit of a joke between me and Dad that Mum sometimes seemed to forget how she had behaved when she was my age. "A right little tease," according to Dad!

Anyway, there I was, the evening before the party, over the moon and all dressed up in my white skirt and top, with Mum going, "Scarlett, I should take that off, if I were you, before you have an accident," and me yelling, "I'm just trying it on!" and Mum retorting,

7

"You've already tried it on a dozen times," and me irritably protesting that, "I have to make sure I feel comfortable in it," when bing, bam, boom! DISASTER. Swishing past the kitchen table, I caught the handle of the coffee pot and that was that. Coffee *all over*. All over me, all over the floor, all over my lovely new outfit. I screeched so loud I'm surprised the neighbours didn't call the police. I couldn't have screeched louder if I'd hacked off my finger with the bread knife. Even Dad heard, and he was outside in the garage. He came bursting in, through the back door.

"What's going on?"

"I told her," said Mum. "I told her to take it off."

Dad said, "Take what off?" And then he caught sight of me covered in coffee and his eyes boggled. "Good grief! What happened?"

"She caught the coffee pot," said Mum.

By this time I was practically hysterical. I am not usually a screechy weepy sort of person, I didn't shed one single tear when I fell over in the playground and broke my wrist, and that was when I was in Year 3. But this was a calamity of cosmic proportions.

"It'll come out," Dad said. "Won't it?"

"Doubt it," said Mum.

"Not even if you put it straight into the machine?"

"Not washable," said Mum. "Has to be dry cleaned."

"Oh, lor'!" said Dad. "Isn't that the get-up she's supposed to be wearing for the party?"

I sobbed, "Yes, but how can I? Now? Look at it! It's ruined! I'll have to go and buy something else! Mum, can I go *straight away* and buy something else?"

"No, I'm afraid you can't," said Mum, at the same time as Dad said, "Well, I suppose—"

"*No*." Mum's lips went all tight and trumpet-shaped. She sounded like she really meant it. "I'm sorry, Scarlett, we'll try taking it to the cleaner's and see what they can do, but—"

"That's no good!" I shrieked at her, like a demented creature. "I need it for tomorrow! Mum, *please*! *Please* let me go and get something else!"

But she wouldn't. She can just be *so* obstinate! Dad was on my side, cos Dad always is, but Mum stood firm. She said I had plenty of other things I could wear, and that I was indulged "quite enough". Dad said, "Isn't that why we have kids? To indulge them?"

"Not to the extent of spoiling them rotten!" snarled Mum.

Poor Dad. What with me weeping and Mum snarling, he looked quite crestfallen. He hates to see me unhappy and he also hates it when Mum gets mad – which just lately she had been doing more and more often. He could obviously tell she wasn't going to give way cos rather lamely he said, "Are you sure it won't come out?" Like he was implying that any proper housewife would know automatically how to remove coffee stains. Which, needless to say, got Mum even madder. She somewhat sniffily informed Dad that she had better ways of occupying her mind than "tedious domestic trivia" and swept out of the room, leaving me

still bleating and Dad looking sheepish, as he always did when Mum turned on him. He told me gruffly to "Cheer up! You know what your mum's like... she'll simmer down." But he didn't say that he was going to overrule her. He didn't tell me to jump in the car and we'd go into town straight away and buy me something else. So that was when I went down into my pit and furiously recorded in my diary that

> *Mum is hateful. She exults in my*
> *misfortune and makes my life a*
> *misery. There are times when it is*
> *just not worth living.*

Like I said, pathetic!

The next day was Saturday, the day of the party. I had already made up my mind to punish Mum by not going. I wanted her to suffer! I'm not quite sure how I thought it was likely to make Mum suffer, me not going to a party that I'd been looking forward to for weeks; I expect I had this vision of her being racked with remorse for ruining my life. I also wanted Dad to

see how desperately miserable I was, cos I knew that me being miserable upset him more than almost anything. But then, while I was still wrapped up in the duvet feeling sorry for myself, Dad put his head round the door and cried, "Wakey, wakey, all systems go! Your mum's had a re-think... I've talked her round."

Three huge cheers for Dad! He was on my side! It was me and Dad versus Mum. Me and Dad were like a team and Mum was like the referee, always blowing her whistle and yelling, "Foul!" We didn't usually take much notice of her. We just did our own thing!

Immediately after breakfast, me and Dad went into town and I went back to the same store. They'd still got the outfit, the same skirt and top, only this time, to be on the safe side in case of more coffee incidents, I got it in a deep emerald green. Dad always said that was my special colour, on account of me having red hair and green eyes, and I knew Tanya wouldn't be wearing it as it doesn't suit her sort of pale faded looks. She always sticks to boring pastel shades like pink (yuck!) and

powder blue. When I got home I said a big thank you to Mum, but Mum just grunted and said, "I don't want to know." I didn't care! I'd got my party clothes and I was back over the moon. Yippee!

Yeah, and guess what? This is my diary entry for the next day:

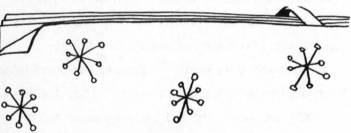

Tanya's stupid party wasn't worth going to. NO boys to speak of, except for just a few geeks, and loads of dim and boring cousins, and people from her old school. I might just as well not have bothered. It was a total waste of a good outfit, cos now everyone's seen me in it, in my beeeeeautiful emerald green skirt and top, I obviously can't wear them again! Not in front of Tanya.

I wonder if I could take them back and change them? I mean, I've only worn them once. They wouldn't know. I could always say they were the wrong size, then I could get one of those tiny little denim jobs that I'd have got last time if Mum hadn't been with me and said they looked tarty. Like she knows anything! What does she know? If she doesn't want me to look tarty she should give me my own clothes allowance and let me get designer gear. But oh, no! that's a RIDICULOUS PRICE, for a girl of your age.

I've just had a look and discovered I can't take the stuff back cos some idiot's gone and dropped a disgusting great splodge of food down the front. I don't know who it

I shall say it again: *pathetic*. OK, I'm not trying to pretend that I don't still think it's important to make the most of yourself. I'm not even trying to pretend that I don't still look forward to parties, and to meeting boys. Course I do! It's only natural. But lots of things have happened to me since I made that entry in my diary. I have been over the moon and down in the dumps and back over the moon and back down in the dumps, up and down, up and down, like a yo-yo, more times than I can remember. I expect that is only natural, too. But I wouldn't ever claim now that my life had been ruined simply on account of *clothes*.

I guess what it is: I have just got older. Older and wiser, as the saying goes. Or, as my best friend Hattie once informed me, in her stern schoolmistressy way, "You have to grow up *some* time." That is it: I have grown up!

Started back at school. Year 8!
We've got Mrs Wymark. She's really
strict, but I think she'll be OK. Me
and Hattie are still together, thank
goodness. Mum says thank
goodness, too. She says I need
Hattie to "quell my worst impulses".
She says if it
weren't for Hattie I
would be like a
walking Barbie doll.
What cheek! Like all
I think about are
clothes, and hair,
and make-up. I
think about loads
of other things! I
said this to Mum, and she said,
"Like what, for instance?" and I said,

cheek!

"Well, boys, for a start. Didn't you used to think about boys?" Dad fell about laughing. He said, "She's got you there!" Mum just said, "Hm".

She pretended to be amused, but I could tell she was wishing that Dad wouldn't get all jokey when she wanted to be serious. I don't know what the matter is with Mum just lately, she's no fun at all. She is becoming really crotchety. Me and Dad, we laugh and fool around the whole time. Everything with Mum is like some big deal. She doesn't seem to have any sense of humour any more. Dad only has to make some totally harmless little joke, like he did the other day, about how women ought to stay home and look after their men instead of having ideas "above their station", and she flies at him like a wildcat. It was only a JOKE, for heaven's sake! I just don't know what's got into her.

That was what I wrote way back last September. Only ten months ago, but it seems like for ever. Reading through my diary is like delving into ancient history. Not that I keep a real proper diary; I don't fill in all the pages. Just now and then, when I feel inspired, I'll pick up a pen and jot things down. I personally consider that I do quite enough writing as it is, what with school all day and homework half the night. I wouldn't have the patience to do more than just scribble the odd few sentences.

Unlike Hattie, who has an actual blog. She spends hours on the computer, setting down her thoughts. She writes these whole long screeds, all about the current political situation and the state of the world. I guess I am more interested in the state of my emotions. I certainly wouldn't want to go putting them on the computer for everyone to read. No way! I would shrivel up and die.

Not even Hattie is allowed to see what I write in my diary. When we were younger we never used to have secrets from each other; we took a vow that we would tell each other *everything*. But the older you get, the more private you get, or at least that is how it seems to me. I surely can't be the only one to keep my innermost thoughts and feelings locked away inside myself? Mostly it's because I'd be embarrassed if I were to tell anyone, but also, maybe, sometimes, it's because I'd be a bit ashamed. I mean, some of the things I think… I know they are not worthy. Like this that I wrote about Tanya Hoskins:

> That girl is so PASTRY-faced. How can anyone say she's pretty??? She looks like she's made out of dough!

Raging jealousy, that's all it was. I've always been jealous of Tanya, right from when we started in Year 7. I knew immediately that she was going to be my rival.

Cos she *is* pretty, in spite of being pale. I was used to being the prettiest one! I always was, in Juniors. I am not saying this to boast; it just happens to be true. Like Hattie was always the cleverest, and Janice McNiece was the best at games. There is no point in denying these things, you have to accept them. What I couldn't accept was that some people might think Tanya Hoskins was as pretty as I was. Not *prettier*; no one could have said she was prettier. But *as* pretty. Oh, this is so hateful! This is what I mean about being ashamed. But I am trying very hard to face up to myself and be truthful. I'm just telling it like it was.

Like it was: I couldn't bear the thought of Tanya being selected for the Founder's Day Dinner and Dance and not me!

There: I said it. That is how petty I was. Of course, I didn't tell Hattie. What I told Hattie was that I really really really *really* wanted to be selected, "Just to show Mum."

Hattie said, "Really?" I said, "Really, really!"

"Dunno how you're going to swing that," said Hattie.

Neither did I; that was the problem. The Dinner and

Dance is a big thing at our school, Dame Elizabeth's. It only happens once every five years, and only a handful of people are selected from each year group, usually five boys and five girls. The way they're chosen is strictly on merit marks – which I didn't happen to have any of. Well, I think I'd picked up about four in the whole of my first year. Hattie, needless to say, got them by the bucket load. Mainly academic ones, since Hattie just happens to have this mega-size brain. Tanya Hoskins has a brain of more ordinary proportions, but she is one of those irritating people who *applies herself.*

(A term much favoured by teachers, at our school at any rate. I always got end-of-term reports saying that I did *not* apply myself.)

"So how do you think you're going to do it?" said Hattie. She is always very down to earth. Not to mention *blunt*.

I said hopefully, "I could try mending my ways."

"Well, you could," said Hattie. "But there's an awful lot of them to mend!"

I begged her not to be so negative. "You're supposed to be helping me!"

"Why?" said Hattie.

"Because you're my friend! And we do things together. How could you possibly go without me?"

"What makes you think I will be going?" said Hattie.

I told her that she was bound to be selected. "You and Tanya; you'll both be selected. You know you will!"

"I don't know anything," said Hattie. "And if you want to go as badly as all that, why not wait for one of the boys to invite you? Cos you know that they will!"

She meant one of the boys who got selected. I said, "*I* want to be the one to do the inviting! Plus there isn't a single solitary boy that I'd want to go with. Not in our year, at any rate."

"So who would you invite?"

I said, "I don't know! I'll think about that later. What's important is *being selected*. And that's what I need your help for!"

"Don't see what I'm s'pposed to do," said Hattie; but she agreed, in the end, to give me the benefit of her advice. "Provided you *listen*."

"I will, I will!" I said. "Look at me… I'm listening!"

"Right, then," said Hattie. "Let's get started. Let's make a list!"

I said, "List of what?"

"All those areas where you need to improve! Get a pen. Write it down!"

Meekly, I did so. "Improvements", I wrote.

No.1 Work

No.2 Behaviour

No.3 Attitude

No.4 Punctuality

No.5 Team spirit.

Somewhat daunting, I think you will agree!

"Let's take them one by one," said Hattie. She has this very orderly sort of mind. "*Work*. If you just started to do some, it would help."

"I will," I said, earnestly.

"You've got a brain," said Hattie, "why not use it?"

I told her that she sounded like my mum.

"I'm going to act like your mum," said Hattie. "I'm going to tell you what to do and you're going to do it… cos if you don't, then that is it. I shall wash my hands of you."

"Oh, no, please," I said. "Please, Hattie, don't!"

"It's entirely up to you," said Hattie. "What's next? *Behaviour*. Well, that's easy enough! Just stop getting told off all the time. *Attitude*—"

"Yes," I said, anxiously, "what does that mean?"

"It means co-operating," said Hattie. "Like, you know… shutting up when you're told to shut up? Walking down the corridor when you're told to walk down the corridor? Not barging and yelling and—"

"I don't do that!" I said.

Hattie looked at me, rather hard.

"Well, yes, all right," I said. "I get the message. What about *punctuality*? I can manage punctuality! At least I can if Dad leaves on time. He doesn't always leave on time."

"So go by train," said Hattie.

The train meant getting up earlier, but I knew if I said that she would just tell me not to be lazy and that "nothing comes without a struggle". And I really really *did* want to be selected! I mean, apart from anything else, it was a matter of pride.

Humbly, I said, "What about *team spirit*? I don't quite get that one."

Hattie said that team spirit meant joining things. Volunteering for things. Trying out for netball teams and hockey teams. I stared at her, appalled.

"You don't do any of that!"

"I'm in the choir," said Hattie.

I wouldn't have minded being in the choir. Unfortunately, I can't sing. Tanya can, of course: very gently and

sweetly. She always gets to do the solos when it's anything holy. Hattie has a voice like a bullhorn. She really belts it out! I would love to have a voice like Hattie's.

"Look, it doesn't matter if you don't get in," said Hattie. "Just *show willing*. That's all you have to do. Then," she added, kindly, "you might get merit marks for general improvement."

Doubtfully I said, "Do they count?"

"Of course they count! They're merit marks, aren't they?"

I said, "Y – yes, I suppose. But I'd need thousands!"

"So get thousands."

She made it sound so easy. She told me to "Look at it this way… nobody, but *nobody*, has as much room for

27

improvement as you. You could get marks for improvement in every single area! Go for it, girl!" I staggered as she biffed me on the shoulder. She packs a hefty punch, does Hattie. "You could wipe the board! So long as you do what I tell you. OK?"

Weakly I said, "OK."

"OK!" She biffed me again, on the other shoulder. "Get started!"

That very same day I added my name to every single list I could find on the notice board. Under–14 netball, Under–14 hockey. Gym, football, basketball. I didn't actually make any of the teams, but at least I had *shown willing*. I just hoped the right people were taking note. I pictured Miss Allen, in the staff room, saying, "Scarlett Maguire is trying so hard this term. She's not really a sporty type, but my goodness, she's giving it a go!"

I didn't try out for swimming cos Tanya is on the swimming team and I didn't want to look stupid in front of her. I mean, I can just barely manage a length doing

the doggy paddle. I did try for the choir (truly squirm-making!) and I also volunteered to paint scenery for the drama club, who fortunately said thank you very much but they didn't need anyone to paint scenery that term as they were doing a production in the round and there wasn't any scenery to be painted. After that, Hattie said that I had probably shown enough team spirit for the time being.

"You don't want to overdo it, it'll be too obvious. They'll think you're just trying to get selected."

"I am," I said.

"No, you're not," said Hattie. "You're having a complete re-think. Change of heart. Reformed character!"

Somewhat alarmed, I assured her that I was exactly the same character I had always been. "All this change of heart stuff… it's only temporary!"

"That's what you think," said Hattie.

What did she know?

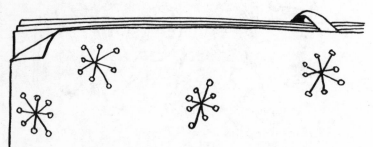

All this effort is really draining me. Paying attention. Showing willing. Doing homework. I can't relax for even two seconds without Hattie's beady eye zooming in on me. This morning I was so utterly exhausted that I drifted off in the middle of French. Just a quick nap – Mrs Kershaw would never have noticed. But before I know it Hattie's angrily jabbing at me with a ruler from across the gangway, pulling a face like a demented gargoyle. Then when I got in a perfectly justifiable strop with Mr Hinckley, who has had the  nerve to give us a THIRD LOT OF HOMEWORK in the same week, she stamped on my foot under the desk and hissed, "Attitude!" I felt like stamping right back, but just in time I happened to catch sight of Tanya simpering away on the other side of  the room like a little saintly sunbeam, so instead of stamping I thought very hard of Founder's Day and stretched my lips into a big smile of gratitude and anticipation, like, thank you SO MUCH, dear, DEAR Mr Hinckley! I am SO looking forward to

doing yet another load of history
homework!

I really don't know if I can stand
the pace. I am already worn to a
frazzle.

Mum was hugely impressed when I started settling
down to my homework every evening without any of
the usual nagging. The *Scarlett-what-about-your-
homework-I-can't-believe-you've-already-done-it-and-
don't-try-telling-me-you-haven't-got-any* kind of thing.
Leading, inevitably, to Big Bust Ups. Resentment and
surliness (according to Mum) on my part, and frayed
temper on hers.

"This is so good!" she said. "I'm so pleased! I know
it's a lot of hard work, but Scarlett, it is *so* important."

To which I responded with a churlish grunt. I mean,
I knew it was churlish but I didn't want Mum exulting
too much; it could only lead to disappointment. This
was not the real me! This was just a temporary kind of
me. I was glad that Mum was happy, but I feared it was
going to make it all the harder when we went back to
frayed tempers.

While Mum approved, Dad wasn't quite so sure. I

could tell he was a bit puzzled by the new me and all the
sudden sunshine radiating from Mum. He was more
used to him and me being in league against her, like
winking and joking and taking the mickey when she
was trying to be serious. He told me that I didn't want
to work *too* hard.

"You know what they say... all work and no play!"

"Frank, for goodness' sake," said Mum. "Don't
discourage her!"

"Well, but she's at it every night," said Dad. "For
crying out loud, what do they expect of these kids?"

"She's got a lot of catching up to do," said Mum.
"She spent the whole of her first year messing around...
I'm just glad she's come to her senses in time."

Dad muttered, "In time for what?"

I said, "In time for Founder's Day!"

Mum got it immediately. There aren't any flies on Mum! "Oh," she said, "so that's what it's all about… I might have known there was an ulterior motive!"

Dad still hadn't caught on. He said, "What's Founder's Day got to do with it?"

"The Dinner and Dance?" said Mum.

"I want so much to go!" I said.

"Well, you will," said Dad. "Of course you will!"

"Not if she's not selected," said Mum.

"She'll be selected!"

"Dad," I said, "I *won't.*"

"What do you mean, you won't? Don't sell yourself short!"

"Frank, they do it on merit," said Mum. "Merit marks. Right?"

"So? She can get merit marks! Brains aren't the only thing. What about looks? Don't they count for something?"

Dad was just blustering; it's what he always does when he's pushed into a corner. Mum made an impatient tutting sound and turned away.

"You don't get merit marks for the way you look," I said.

"Well, you darned well ought to!" said Dad. "You'd be a credit to the school!"

I said, "Hattie will be a credit to the school."

"In her own way," said Dad. "In her own way."

He knew better than to come straight out and say anything derogatory about Hattie's looks; Mum would have been down on him like a ton of bricks. It's true that Hattie is not beautiful. It is also true that she is a rather *solid* kind of person. Sort of square-shaped. But she has a really good face, very strong and full of character, and it wasn't kind of Dad to say some of the things that he did. He never dared in front of Mum, cos he knew she wouldn't stand for it, but sometimes when it was just him and me he'd have these little digs like, "Poor old Hat, she's as broad as she is long!" Or one time, I remember, he said that she would make a great sumo wrestler, which is totally unfair, as sumo wrestlers are fat. Hattie is *not fat.*

It always used to make me feel uncomfortable: really disloyal to Hattie. I know I should have said something.

35

I should have told Dad that I didn't like him making these sort of remarks about my best friend; but I never did. Cos me and Dad were in league. We used to point people out to each other when we went anywhere, like when Dad drove me to school in the morning. "Good grief!" Dad would go. "Get a load of that!" Or I would say, "Just look what that girl is wearing! Some people have *no* dress sense!"

It was our thing that we did; we enjoyed it. Mum said it was very superficial, judging others by the way they looked, but me and Dad never took any notice. We just laughed.

All the same, I did agree with Mum on one thing: I certainly didn't need Dad discouraging me from doing my homework. I was having enough of a struggle as it was.

Mum said to me later that I mustn't let Dad put me off.

"You know he has a problem with women asserting themselves."

I really didn't think I could be accused of asserting myself, just doing my homework, but Mum reminded me how Dad had been brought up. *His* mum had been quite old when he was born and had these really old-fashioned views, like a woman's place being in the home and men not having to lift a finger to help with domestic chores. Dad wasn't as bad as that, but I had to admit, he wasn't exactly a modern man.

"You just stick to your guns," said Mum. "I don't care what your reasons are; anything that motivates you has to be a good thing. I'm speaking here from experience. It's taken me the better part of thirty years to get motivated. I wasted a large chunk of my life, I'd hate to see you waste yours."

I wasn't sure what Mum meant when she said about wasting her life. She'd got married, she'd had me, she'd helped Dad build up the business. When they'd started out he'd been a penniless nobody; now he owned his own company. How could Mum say that was a waste?

"What was a waste," said Mum, "was leaving school

at sixteen with no qualifications. It severely limits your choices. They say it's never too late, but take it from me... the longer you leave it, the harder it becomes. So please, Scarlett, I know you love your dad, I know you're his pride and joy, but *don't let him talk you out of it*! OK?"

I said OK, feeling a bit shaken – Mum had never spoken to me like this before, I'd had no idea how she felt – but I wailed at Hattie later that week that I didn't seem to be getting anywhere. Hattie, in her sensible way, said it was because I was out of practice. She said, "You've lost the habit. Don't worry! It'll come back."

Glumly I said, "If I ever had it in the first place."

"Well, you did," said Hattie, "cos I remember once you beat me in a spelling test and I was jealous for simply days."

I said, "Really?" It cheered me up for about a second, but then I lapsed once again into gloom. I told

Hattie that it must have been a fluke. "Either that or I cheated."

"You didn't cheat! You didn't need to. Miss Marx once said you were one of her best pupils."

I said, "Miss Marx was in Year 2!"

"Year 3, actually," said Hattie.

"Well, anyway." I was feeling particularly down that day. I had just had a piece of homework returned with *Unsatisfactory!* scrawled at the bottom of it in rude red ink. I didn't mind getting bad marks when I hadn't bothered to work, but I had spent hours on that essay. It was very dispiriting; I had always thought I was in control of my life. I wasn't used to being inadequate.

"I don't know why I'm bothering," I said. "I obviously haven't got enough brain cells."

"That," said Hattie, "is one of the most insulting things you have ever said to me."

"What???" I blinked. "What are you talking about? I'm not insulting you!"

"Yes, you are! You're saying that I have chosen to be best friends with a moron. Well, thank you very much! Do you think it's *likely*," said Hattie, "that you and me would still be hanging out with each other if that were the case? People without brains," said Hattie (she is prone to making these kind of sweeping statements) "are just totally dead *boring*."

I told her that that was a horrible thing to say. "People can't help whether they have brains or not."

"They can help whether they *use* them or not."

I said, "Huh!"

"Don't you go huh to me," said Hattie. "I know you, Scarlett Maguire! You think just because you're pretty you can swan through life without bothering, but this time you can't! Not if you really really really want to go to Founder's Day!"

It is terrible, how well Hattie knows me. And the

40

things she dares to say! She only gets away with it because we have been friends for so long. She is always right, of course; that is what makes her so absolutely maddening!

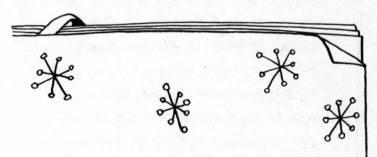

Bumped into Mrs O'Donnell on the way home from school today. She asked me how I was getting on. It seems she'd heard from Mum that I was desperate to be selected for Founder's Day. I wish Mum wouldn't go round telling people! It will be just soooo humiliating when it doesn't happen.

I told Mrs O'Donnell that I wasn't holding out much hope, and she said how you never know your luck and to keep at it. "Work hard! That's the ticket."

What *does* she mean, that's the ticket? What ticket? Ticket to Founder's Day? I don't think so. I said this to Mrs O'Donnell. I said, "I really don't stand an earthly... who wants to go, anyway? It's only a status thing." At which Mrs O'Donnell got excited and screeched out, really loud, in that embarrassing way that she has, telling me that I'd got it all wrong, it was a lovely, lovely event!

It turns out that she was there, about a hundred years ago. Mrs O'Donnell, at the Founder's Day Dinner! Un-be-lieveable! She's said I can go round and look at her photos if I want, so I think I might. It would be interesting to see her as a young girl... I can't imagine it!

That was an entry I made shortly after my conversation with Hattie, when she had a go at me for not using my brain. Hattie had sort of bucked me up, a little bit, but I was still feeling sore about that *unsatisfactory* scrawled at the bottom of my homework.

I just couldn't see that I was ever going to get enough merit marks. All this effort, and all for nothing! And then I bumped into Mrs O'Donnell and everything changed.

Mrs O'Donnell is this big jolly person that lives near us. I knew she'd been to Dame Elizabeth's some time back in the dark ages, cos she was always telling me about it, but I never knew she'd been selected for Founder's Day. It came as a bit of a shock, to be quite honest. Like, *Mrs O'Donnell*? *How special is she*? Pur-lease! She may be extremely pleasant and friendly, but there is absolutely nothing exceptional about her. Not as far as I can see.

I made the mistake of saying this to Mum, who rolled her eyes and said, "There you go! Making judgements again."

I said, "But she's never done anything!"

"How do you know?" said Mum. "How do you know *what* Mrs O'Donnell may or may not have done?"

I didn't, of course. All I knew was that she was a fat woman with a grown-up family and a husband who played golf with my dad. But I went to look at her

43

photographs, just out of curiosity, and I got another
shock, cos when she was my age Mrs O'Donnell was
really skinny and attractive, and Mr O'Donnell, who is
now completely bald and looks, when seen from a
bedroom window, like
an egg going up the
road, had gorgeous
thick hair, very black

and wavy. Mrs
O'Donnell, no doubt
sensing my utter
astonishment, said,
"Oh, yes, he was a dish!" Well, I like to
please people when I can, so I enthusiastically agreed,
saying that he was really fit, cos I guessed that's what
she'd meant by saying he was a dish. Unfortunately, it
was like we spoke in different languages. Mrs O'Donnell
said, "He was fit, right enough! Used to run cross-
country for the school… and old fat woman here used to
play hockey for the first eleven, if you can imagine that!"

I couldn't. I just *could not* identify the Mrs O'Donnell that I knew with the girl in the photograph. Altogether it was a sobering experience and made me reflect on what time does to people. But it also renewed my flagging spirits. In spite of Hattie and her bullying ways, I'd almost been on the point of giving up. I mean, three lots of history homework in one week, I ask you! It was the photograph of Mrs O'Donnell at Founder's Day with her beau that did it. That's what she called him: her beau! In other words, Mr O'Donnell, dressed to kill with all his hair. They had been young and beautiful once, just like me!

Mrs O'Donnell said, "Those were the days… " She told me to make the most of my youth while I had it, "Because once it's gone, it's gone." I get really uncomfortable when old people start talking like that. I don't like to think of myself all lumpy and shapeless and saggy-bummed! As quick as I could, I got her off the subject and asked her, instead, how she'd managed to get enough merit marks.

She said, "For Founder's Day, you mean? I'll tell you the secret: I knuckled down. True as I stand here… I worked hard, I played hard, and I resisted temptation."

"Was it a struggle?" I said.

"Nearly killed me! But I was absolutely determined to

be chosen and that was for one reason and one reason only: so that I could ask Jack O'Donnell to come as my partner." She nodded at me, and winked, like it was the two of us in some kind of conspiracy against the opposite sex. "Never knew what hit him, poor man! How about you? Who are you planning to ask?"

I told her that I hadn't really thought that far ahead.

"Come on!" she said. "You expect me to believe that? A pretty girl like you? You could take your pick!"

I always used to preen when people said things like that to me, I really basked in admiration. Now I find it quite embarrassing; I am nowhere near as vain as I used to be. But what Mrs O'Donnell said started me furiously thinking, so that that night in bed I lay awake making a mental list of all the boys I knew, scoring them out of ten, trying to decide which one I would pick if I ever got to be selected.

Jason Francis – not bad. Six or seven.

Martin Milliband – yuck! Two would be generous.

Aaron Taylor – OK, but a bit of a dork. Five at the most.

Christopher Pitts – *the* pits. Zero. *Double* zero.

Wazir Mohammed – probably wouldn't come. But five or six.

Carl Pinter, Mark Aller, Ben Sargent… I think I went through every boy in our year. I'd been out with quite a few of them and I wouldn't have wanted to invite a single solitary one. I knew who I'd like to invite. I'd known it the minute I started my list – the minute Mrs O'Donnell asked me. The one boy who made my heart beat faster and turned my insides to jelly…

There was only one problem: I didn't know his name. I'd never even spoken to him! But I made up my mind, right there and then: I *was* going to be selected, and he was the one who was going to come with me!

This is the first entry in my diary which mentions the Gorgeous Mystery Boy:

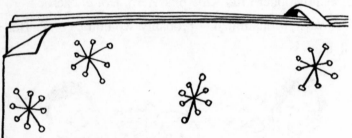

Mrs Wymark said to me today that she was really pleased with my progress this term. She said, "There's been a marked improvement, Scarlett. Keep it up!" She said she wasn't the only member of staff to have noticed. They all have! So maybe I was right when I pictured Miss Allen singing my praises in the staff room…

I really began to feel that all my hard work might be starting to pay off at long last. I said this to Hattie, who said, "I told you so!" Adding rather grimly, however, that it was no excuse for slacking. "You need to keep it up, you still have a long way to go."

Honestly! Hattie is so bossy, I'm sure she'll end up as a head teacher. Either that, or prime minister. I

don't know what I shall end up as. I wouldn't mind being a fashion model, or a TV presenter. If I was a TV presenter and Hattie was prime minister, I could invite her to come on my show! But

We were four weeks into the winter term when I
wrote that. Dad had proved so unreliable about getting
me to school on time that now I just got him to drop me
off at the station, instead. When I was at Juniors, Mum
used to drive me in, but the minute I hit Year 7 she said
that I could get there under my own steam.

"There's a perfectly good train service. Why not use it?"

I told her because it was a whole lot of hassle and I'd
probably have some ghastly accident and fall on the
track. Mum, in her cold unfeeling way, said, "Well,
that's up to you. I don't propose adding to pollution
levels by ferrying an able-bodied twelve year old to and
from school five days a week."

Was that any way for a mother to talk??? I went
grizzling to Dad about it.

"Mum says she's not going to take me in any more and I'm going to have all these books and things to carry, cos they give you absolutely *masses* of homework, plus there's my hockey stick, plus that *stupid* violin, which was Mum's idea, not mine, plus it takes for ever to get to the station… I'm going to be worn out before I even get there!"

Dad said we couldn't have that; he said that he would take me. But Dad isn't one of the world's great timekeepers. I don't think builders are, cos I once heard two woman talking on a bus, saying what a nightmare it was when you "had the builders in". How they never turned up when they said they would turn up, and never finished a job when they said they'd finish a job, and how they were "all alike… they simply have no concept of time".

That's my dad! I used to think it was
probably me, as well, but it is amazing
what a bit of an incentive can do. A
*double* incentive, in my case, cos
once I'd spotted the Gorgeous
Mystery Boy I couldn't get up
to the station fast enough
each day. Dad didn't know
what had hit him. There
was me going, "Dad,
come on, I've got a
train to catch!"
"Dad, *please*, I'll
be late!" and
Dad going,
"All right,
all right!

What's all the big rush? So you miss one train, you get the next." It's true there are trains like about every ten minutes from Ritters Cross to Hayes End at that time in the morning, but the way I saw it, the earlier I was there, the more chance I had of Catching a Glimpse. I mean, let's face it, there aren't so many gorgeous boys knocking around that you can afford to let one slip through your fingers, as it were.

Bullying Dad really paid off. I not only arrived at school on time, thus earning merit marks for punctuality (me! Merit marks for punctuality!!!) I also got to catch not one but several glimpses of the divine being. The Gorgeous Mystery Boy. I relayed it all excitedly to Hattie. She was like, "Tell me, tell me! Colour of hair?"

I said, "Gold... *really* gold, you know?"

Hattie said, "Gold like gold, or gold like yellow?"

I said, "Gold like gold! Not yellow. Yuck! And not just ordinary blond. Gold like... molten sunshine!"

Hattie said, "Ooh! Nice. Go on! Eyes?"

"Blue," I said.

"Blue. Wow! Tall or short?"

Proudly, I said, "Tall!"

"Fat or thin?"

"*Athletic*."

"Which school?"

"Grove Park."

"Mm…" Hattie pulled a face. "Could be worse."

I said that it could have been a lot worse. Grove Park might have a bit of a tough reputation but at least it's all boys. I said this to Hattie and she said, "I take your point… no opposition!"

Although Hattie isn't – well, wasn't – into boys in as big a way as I was, it's never stopped us having these long heart-to-hearts on the subject. For all her great brain, Hattie can get just as girly and giggly as I can. She begged to be allowed to see my new "dream guy".

"Where can I get a look at him?"

I said she should wait for me next morning at the ticket barrier. We don't usually meet up, as Hattie comes in from the opposite direction and the trains don't coincide, but she said that tomorrow she would catch an earlier one and hang about.

"I'll just hover. I won't be obvious!"

"You can't miss him," I said. I got this hot fizzy

feeling inside me just talking about him. *Zing, pop, sizzle*, like a bottle of Coke exploding. I told Hattie that sometimes he was with a friend, another boy from Grove Park. I think I sort of half had in mind that maybe the friend would do for Hattie. She could sigh over him, and I could sigh over the Gorgeous Mystery Boy. It would be more fun if we could sigh together; I didn't like the thought of Hattie being left out.

She wanted to know what the friend was like. I said he was OK, but the truth was I hadn't really paid much attention to him.

"Hair?"

"Dark."

"Eyes?"

"Dunno."

"Tall or short?"

"Tall. Ish."

"Fat or thin?"

"Thin."

"You mean... thin like weedy, or thin like athletic?"

"Not athletic. I think he's got something wrong with him."

"Wrong how?"

"I dunno, he has this trouble walking."

"Like… sprained ankle, maybe?"

"Dunno. Don't think so. Think it's more than that."

"Hm." Hattie crinkled her brow, as she considered the problem. "Congenital?"

Whatever that meant. It sounded vaguely rude to me.

"Something he was *born* with," said Hattie. "Like a club foot or something?"

I said again that I didn't know. I didn't find the subject anywhere near as fascinating as Hattie appeared to, but she tends to be a tidge on the ghoulish side. She loves to dwell on morbid details, like when they have medical programmes on the telly and she is absolutely glued to them.

"Be there tomorrow," I said, "and you can see for yourself."

Hattie promised that she would. She said that I needed an eye kept on me and that she was the person to do it, but really and truly, I could tell, she was just bursting with vulgar curiosity!

Hattie has caught her first glimpse! She was there by the barrier this morning – loitering with intent – and he walked right past her. Literally within centimetres. They might even have touched. Hattie agrees with me that he is totally out of this world! We have been trying to work out which year he is likely to be in; we think probably Year 10. Hattie says he has to be at least fourteen and could even be fifteen. In other words, just right! I don't go for little boys. This is why there is no one in our class that I would even consider asking to partner me on Founder's Day. If I am selected, that is. Oh, but I have to be! I just have to be! Especially now. I mean, now that I know who I am

going to ask ... cos I will ask! I'll find
a way.

His friend was there this morning,
the one who walks with a limp.
Hattie had a look and says it is not
a club foot. She wonders if perhaps
he has had polio, but I didn't think
people got polio these days.
Whatever it is, it makes him walk in a
very odd way, so that he has
difficulty keeping up. We have
christened them Peg Leg and the
Sun God!

In fact it was Hattie who thought up the name Sun God and me who thought of Peg Leg. I am quite ashamed of it now, but I didn't know his name and I had to call him something. Hattie disapproved even at the time. She said he hadn't got a peg leg, just a limp.

"And you don't refer to people with disabilities by their disability!"

I said, "I don't see why not, if you don't know their name."

"Because it's rude and insensitive," said Hattie. "It's *discriminatory*."

She's always using these words. She doesn't do it to show off, it just comes naturally to her; she's like a talking dictionary. It is very educational, having Hattie for a friend. But that doesn't stop me arguing with her!

"I'm not being dis—" *Damn.* I couldn't say it properly. "I'm not being!"

"Yes, you are," said Hattie. "You just don't realise it. It's like when the police describe suspects as black. *That's* discriminatory."

She is always so politically correct! It gets on my nerves at times. I told her that it wasn't discriminatory at all. "It's just a way of identifying people... I wouldn't mind if someone called me *the girl with red hair*."

Hattie said that was because I was secretly proud of having red hair.

I said, "Well, black people are probably proud of being black."

"Yeah? I don't expect they'd be proud of walking with a limp!"

I said, "All right, so how would you describe him? Like when we're talking, what would you call him? Friend of Sun God?"

Hah! That stumped her. I don't very often get one over on Hattie, but this time she didn't have an answer. She came back to it later, when we were walking round together at break. Hattie is like a dog with a bone. She can worry a subject to death.

"I wouldn't just call him Friend of Sun God. He's a person in his own right. He has to have a name of his own."

"OK," I said, "so what would you call him?"

"I'm going to call him Hermes," said Hattie.

I said, "Who's Hermes? Pardon my ignorance."

"Pardon granted," said Hattie. "Hermes was the messenger of the gods. It's kind of how I picture him… thin, and dark."

"Wouldn't be much of a messenger," I said. "Wouldn't get anywhere very fast!"

I suppose it wasn't really funny. Hattie gave me this withering look. "Ever heard of mass communications? I bet he's a computer whiz. He looks like he's got a brain."

"What, and Sun God hasn't?"

"Did I say that?" said Hattie.

"You implied it."

"I did not! He might be an academic genius, for all I know."

"But you don't really think he is… just cos he's totally gorgeous you think he's a moron! Now who's being discriminating?"

We argued – quite amicably – all through break. Me and Hattie are always having these kind of spats.

It's mostly Hattie who starts them. It has to be said, she's a very disputatious sort of person; really quite opinionated. But I do enjoy the cut and thrust of intellectual debate.

The name Hermes didn't really stick, though it was strange Hattie should have chosen it. (For explanation, see later!) Privately, in my diary, I still referred to him as Peg Leg, while in conversation the Sun God mostly became "you-know-who" – accompanied by a lovesick sigh. Hattie either called him Apollo or sometimes just God, when she wanted to be sarcastic or make fun of me.

I guess I did get a bit drippy. Very tiresome, as I know from experience. Hattie once got drippy over this beastly boring cricket person that she couldn't stop going on about. I mean, cricket, for heaven's sake! Fortunately it was just a phase she was going through; she's out of it now. But I was still at the stage where I had these mad explosions going off every time I opened my mouth, like a thousand sparklers all fizzing and hissing.

"I just wish I knew his name," I wailed.

Hattie agreed that knowing his name would be an advantage. "Unless, of course, it turns out to be something like Wayne, or Kevin, or—"

"It won't, it won't!" *Please* let it not be. Not Wayne or Kevin!

"Marmaduke. Alistair. *George*—"

"Shut up!" I said. "You're making me feel ill!"

"How about Sebastian? How about—"

"Oh, Hattie, do be quiet!" I said. "Listen, guess what? I got a merit mark for history! That's ten already... if I get selected – *if* I get selected – I could invite you-know-who to be my partner!"

"Well, yes," said Hattie, "if you ever get around to talking to him. Or would you just go waltzing up out of the blue and say, 'Hi! Want to come to Founder's Day with me?'"

"I'm going to get to know him," I said. "Don't worry! I'm working on it. In any case, there's ages to go. They don't do the selection till some time next term."

"Omigawd," said Hattie. "Don't tell me... another three months of inane burble!"

Although I'd said that I was "working on it", the truth was I didn't have any sort of strategy in mind. I guess I was secretly hoping that just being around, on the platform, every morning at the same time would be enough to get me noticed. I mean, I'd noticed him; he could notice me! This probably sounds extremely conceited, but I knew I was noticeable cos my hair is not just red, it's more like flame coloured. And our school uniform is green, which really suits me. Dad always said that if I'd been sent to Hayes High he'd have paid for me to go private rather than see me in their puke-making get-up. It is bright purple!!!

Still, you can't always rely on boys taking note of things like clothes. The fact was, I needed a plan. Some way of drawing attention to myself. Maybe I could... stage a fainting fit right in front of him?

No! That was stupid. I'd learnt enough about boys to know that he wouldn't find it in the least romantic. Boys don't like girls who flake out on them, and anyway, I wasn't the type. I despise people who faint!

Tanya fainted once, during assembly. She had to be carted away to the side of the hall and sat on a chair with her head between her knees. *Not* very becoming!

OK. No fainting. So maybe I could ... tread on his foot and apologise? Abjectly, and with great charm. "Oh, my goodness, I am *so* sorry!"

He probably wouldn't even feel it. Or if he did, he'd just think what a clumsy idiot I was. I didn't want him thinking I was clumsy!

How about if I actually went up to him and asked him if he knew... who? Anyone! Make up a name... Miles Bailey!

"You don't happen to know Miles Bailey, do you?"

And he would say no, why? And I would say... what would I say? I would say, "His sister's a friend of mine! He used to go to your school."

That would be even more stupid than fainting. That would just make me sound desperate.

But I was desperate! I had to find *some* way of getting to know him. And then, while I was still agonising, chance came to my rescue, as chance so often does. What I am saying is, I think you have to be prepared – like in my case being *on time* every single day for positively weeks; but then in the end you need a bit of luck, cos it's luck that creates opportunities. You just have to be ready to jump in at the right moment!

This is what I wrote in my diary:

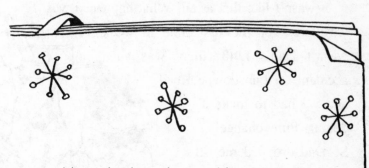

I have broken the ice. I have spoken to Peg Leg! We sat on the train together and talked. His name

is Simon, and the Sun God is Matt.
Such a relief! I was getting really
scared in case it was something
naff, like Wayne or Alan. I HATE the
name Alan! But Matt is cool. He's
off school at the moment on some
field trip, so I won't see him for a
while. How am I going to survive???
Two whole weeks without him! But at
least now I've introduced myself.

Don't you just love the way I said that? "Introduced myself", like it was so polite and formal? Like, "Good morning, how do you do? I'm Scarlett Maguire, I don't believe we've spoken before."

It wasn't like that at all! What happened was, I was *late*. For the first time in weeks. It wasn't Dad's fault, there was an accident on Lansdowne Road and we had to make a detour. Pure chance! So Dad dropped me off at the bottom of Station Parade, and there I was, churning my way through a sea of bodies, arms flailing, legs going like piston rods, when lo and behold I tripped over a bit of broken paving stone and went crashing headlong into…

You've got it! Peg Leg. I mean, Simon. (I'm not going to call him Peg Leg any more.

I only wrote it because that was how I still thought of him. But I don't any longer: it makes me cringe, now, to remember that I ever did.)

Poor boy! He was sent flying. It's not that I'm particularly heavy (I take after Mum, I'm naturally quite slim) but when you have one leg that is shorter than the other you are not very well balanced. God, I felt so awful! He dropped his bag and stuff went shooting off in all directions. It was very embarrassing. But as I scrabbled around, collecting things up, I couldn't resist a quick peek at his name on one of the books: Simon Carson. Year 10.

Needless to say, I did my abject apologising. For real, this time! He was really nice about it. I mean, he could have been quite sniffy, having a human cannon ball come walloping into him, but he said not to worry. "It happens." As we walked into the station together, I reflected that if it had been the Sun God I'd bashed into, I would have been the one sent flying, not the Sun God. And it occurred to me, a mean and nasty little snippet of a thought sliding into the outer edges of my consciousness, that Simon and the Sun God were a bit like me and Hattie. I am almost too ashamed to explain, but I have to remind myself that I am still trying to tell it like it was. I made a vow that I would not do a whitewash job. Otherwise, I mean, what is the point?

OK. Deep breath… Simon was a cripple, the Sun God was divine, Hattie was a solid lump and I was—

It's no use, I can't say it. It's just not me, I don't think that way any more.

*I am a changed person!*

I think there are limits to the amount of mortification a person can be expected to inflict on themselves. I shall just quietly get on with the story.

Once I'd knocked him over, and picked up his books, and said that I was sorry, it seemed only natural we should get on the train together; and as we were standing shoulder to shoulder, wodged in on all sides, it would have been a bit odd not to talk. What we mostly

talked about was school, and stuff we'd seen on telly, and whether we were going to a gig that was happening at the Landsdowne Centre; and then as we pulled into Hayes End I couldn't resist it, I said, "What's happened to your friend? The one you usually come in with?" And he smiled, like he was used to people being more interested in his friend than they were in him, and told me that Matt had gone off on this field trip to Snowdonia.

"So you won't be seeing him for a while."

Fortunately we were getting off the train at the time, so he wouldn't have noticed my cheeks going bright red to match my hair. I was like, "Oh, I just wondered," making it sound really casual, like I'd only asked in order to make conversation. I don't think he was fooled,

though, cos he smiled again and said, "Yeah, sure." Very belittling! But I don't honestly think, at the time, that I was aware. I was too cock-a-hoop. I'd done it! I'd talked! I'd found out his name!

*Definitely* an over-the-moon day.

I'm thinking of making these days official. Over-the-moon day, under-the-moon day. Up day, down day. Pits day, dump day. Things-are-looking-up day. I could have little symbols for them, like smileys for the up ones and saddos for the down.

Yeah, well, it's just an idea. It could save a whole lot of time. Instead of writing all those reams in my diary I could just put, like, ☺ over-the-moon! Or ☹ down-in-the-dumps. Then at the end of the year I could add them all up and see how often I'd been UP and how often I'd been DOWN. That would tell me what kind of year it had been.

I think most probably, on the whole, I tend to be more of an UP kind of person. I would say that I was more up than down during those next two weeks. I couldn't wait till Matt returned from his field trip and I could see him again, but meanwhile I was prepared to make do with Simon. I tried my best to be early every morning so's not to miss him. I even took to setting my alarm clock half an hour in advance, then springing out of bed, snatching an apple and a glass of milk, and galloping *on foot* to the station, rather than relying on Dad. That way, at least I could be sure of being there on time. When Simon showed up it was a big SMILEY day. We'd stand together on the train and I'd ask him questions about Matt, like, "Where does he live?" (Ranthorne Avenue) "What's his best subject?" (Sport!) "How long have you known him?" (For ever.)

Occasionally, however, Simon wasn't there, and then it was a DOWN DAY. A total waste. There just didn't seem any point in a day

when I couldn't talk about Matt. I could talk about him to Hattie, of course – which I did, with a vengeance! – but it wasn't the same, because Hattie didn't know him. When I talked about him with Simon I felt as if we were … connected. Almost like I'd been talking to Matt himself. I tried explaining this to Hattie, who shook her head, not unsympathetically, and said, "You've got it real bad, girl!"

And oh, I had. I had!

I was counting the days till Matt came back from his field trip. Actually crossing them off on the calendar. I had a big red arrow pointing to the day when I would see him again. Mum  caught sight of it and asked me what it was for. I said, "Oh! Just something."

"Something nice," said Mum, "by the looks of things."

She was trying really hard! But I wasn't going to tell. Not that Mum would have laughed: she has always been very good like that. She has always taken me seriously, it's Dad who teases. But Hattie was the only one I could

73

talk to about Matt, and the feelings he inspired in me. I dreamt about him every night! I even had my own private soap opera (*Scarlett 'n' Matt*) which I played through in my head while I was supposedly watching telly or eating dinner. I kept adding newer and more exciting episodes. Sometimes it got quite hairy!

One time I was in the middle of an episode when Dad said something to me and I came to with a start. I could feel my cheeks growing all red and hectic. Dad said, "What's up?" which made me grow even redder and even more hectic! How could I possibly tell him? If he knew the thoughts that were going on inside my head he would throw fifty fits on the spot. Dad has always been hugely protective. He likes the idea of boys fancying me, but he tends to get agitated if I actually go out with them. He once saw me holding hands with Aaron Taylor and it almost made him freak. It almost makes me freak, now, but I was only ten at the time... I hadn't yet set eyes on Matt!!!

I dressed *so* carefully the day he was due back. Well, I still had to wear school uniform, of course, but I hitched up the skirt a notch, cos regulation length is truly unflattering, even on me, and I'd washed my hair the night before so that it was all fluffy, and I knew that I was looking really good. Dad noticed. He said, "Who are you off to meet, all done up like a dog's dinner?"

"Just going to school," I said.

I shot out of the house ten minutes early and went whizzing fast as maybe up to the station. I had to let two trains come and go before Simon arrived. I bounced over to him, beaming. I look back, and I can *see* myself beaming. And I can hear myself gushing.

"Hi! Where's Matt?"

Oh, God! Did I have *no* pride?

"Isn't he back yet? I thought he was due back!"

That was when it became Black Monday. Doomsday. Dump day. Down-in-the-pits day. *Matt wasn't there.*

He wasn't ever going to be there again – well, not at the station. He'd moved out to West Whitton to be with his dad.

I think my face must visibly have fallen – Hattie always says that I am totally transparent – cos Simon  very slowly and gently explained to me how Matt had been living with his mum for the past few years, but now his mum had married again and was moving up north, so Matt had opted to live with his dad rather than change schools.

Foolishly, I blethered, "So he won't be coming in with you any more?"

Oh, pur*lease*! I remember that I went all weak and wobbly, like my bones had dissolved into some kind of jelly.

Simon said no, he'd be getting the bus.

"Oh, but won't you miss him?" I bleated.

I can still see the look Simon gave me. It is best described as *pitying*. I knew I was being utterly pathetic, but I just couldn't seem to stop myself. I guess I was suffering from shock. I'd been so looking forward to seeing Matt again, and now he had gone and my life was empty.

"He's still at school," said Simon.

Yes, but not *my* school. I really felt like the bottom had dropped out of my world. I almost felt all over again that there was no point in carrying on with the struggle. (To gain merit marks, that is.) Originally I'd been all fired up cos of wanting to show Tanya. But then I'd seen Matt, and Tanya just didn't figure any more. She just wasn't an issue. The only reason for working hard, and being punctual, and changing my attitude and all the rest, was so that I could go to Founder's Day with Matt as my partner. And now he wasn't there and all incentive had vanished. If I couldn't go with Matt, I didn't want to go with anyone!

I poured out my woes to Hattie, who listened patiently and did her best to cheer me up, telling me that all was not lost, and at least I had Simon. Ungraciously I wailed that I didn't want Simon, I wanted Matt! Hattie told me that Simon was a link, and reminded me that the path of true love never did run smooth.

"You have to fight for these things! They're not just going to fall into your lap."

So then I felt a bit ashamed and apologised for being such a bore, but Hattie said that was all right. She said, "What are friends for?" It's true that I would listen to Hattie if she were ever dealt a mortal blow, and I did try to buck my ideas up, but it was a really bad day. A *really* bad day. I couldn't even bring myself to write about it in my diary. I'd put a big STAR at the top of Monday, in anticipation, cos I'd been so sure it was going to be an over-the-moon day, but when it came to it I wrote just the one word: *Gloom.*

This is what I mean about ups and downs. For the past two weeks I'd been in a bubble, floating high, up amongst the clouds – and now, all of a sudden, without any warning, the bubble had burst and cast me down. Deep into a pit of total depression…

But it is all a merry-go-round, cos three days later, guess what? I was back up!

Met Simon at the station. He
wanted to know if I liked football. I
nearly went no,
yuck, I can't
stand it! I went
once with Dad
and it was just
sooooo boring.

Fortunately, in the nick of time I
remembered Simon telling me that
sport was Matt's best subject, so
instead of saying yuck I went,
"Mmmmm…" in that sing song sort
of way that means – whatever you
want it to mean! In this case, "Well,
yes, maybe, quite. Sometimes." Not
actually committing myself to mad
enthusiasm, but not betraying my
true feelings, either. Which is just as
well cos he told me that Matt is

playing in a match on Saturday and
that if I liked I could go with him and
watch!

Naturally I said that I would. I am
so excited! How boring can it be if
Matt is there???

So there I was, back over-the-moon. Just like that! I
asked Hattie if she would like to come with me. She
didn't really want to, she said she had important stuff to
put on her blog, but I nagged at her, reminding her that
friendship sometimes meant *duty*, like doing things for
each other even if it wasn't madly convenient, so that in
the end she obviously felt ashamed of herself and gave
in. The reason I wanted her there: I had this idea that
after the game we would probably all go off together
somewhere, like the Panino Bar or Jolly's or
somewhere, and Hattie could sit and talk to Simon
while I talked to Matt; but it didn't quite work out that
way. Well, actually, it didn't work out that way at all.

It was just me and Hattie and Simon, because Matt
stayed on with the rest of the team for a general nosh-
up so that I didn't even get to say a proper hallo to him.
That was a bit of a downer; I'd built my hopes up so
high! But while we were sitting in Jolly's, with Simon

and Hattie going on at huge and boring length about the stuff she was going to put on her blog, I suddenly had this brilliant idea and without giving myself time to think, and maybe get embarrassed – because after all it could be said that I was being a trifle pushy – I leaned across the table and shouted, "Would you and Matt like to come to our after-Christmas party?"

I don't know why I shouted: nerves, probably. Hattie looked at me in amazement. Simon seemed a bit startled. He said it was very kind of me to ask, but he didn't really go to parties. I said, "Not go to *parties*?" I'd never met anyone that didn't go to parties! Simon explained that it was because he couldn't dance, which was something that hadn't occurred to me. I suppose it would be quite miserable, just having to sit and watch everyone else, though goodness knows there are lots of other things to do at parties! But anyway, I hastened to reassure him. I said there wasn't likely to be much in the way of dancing.

"It's mostly grown-ups... neighbours and stuff. Aunties and uncles. That sort of thing. It's Dad's special after-Christmas get-together. Dad *invented* it. It's to keep people going between Christmas and New Year... it's quite fun! Hattie always comes, don't you?"

Hattie nodded, without actually saying anything. It occurred to me that she could have been a bit more supportive.

"What we sometimes do," I said, "we sometimes go and mess around in the pool. We've got this indoor pool, it's fun! Isn't it?"

I turned again to Hattie, who said, "I guess so, if you like that kind of thing."

I could have brained her. It's true that Hattie herself, personally, doesn't much care for going in the water, but really! She is supposed to be my *friend*. It was all the excuse Simon needed. He said apologetically that he not only couldn't dance, he didn't swim, either. Frankly I was beginning to feel quite out of patience with both him and Hattie. With my best bright smile, I said, "But Matt does, doesn't he?"

Simon said yes, Matt did. "He's on the school team."

"Well, there you are, then! He'd enjoy it," I said, "wouldn't he?"

Simon said yes, he probably would.

"So you could ask him! Tell him I've invited both of you. If Matt comes, you'll have to come, as well," I said, "to keep Hattie company, cos she's not mad on swimming, either. Are you?"

Hattie shook her head. She seemed kind of resigned; so did Simon. He promised that he would speak to Matt and let me know.

"Talk about *obvious*," said Hattie, when Simon had gone and we were on our way back through the shopping centre.

Loftily I told her that there were times when you had to be.

"Things don't happen all by themselves, you know. You have to do something to help them along."

"Oh, absolutely," said Hattie. But I felt that I detected a note of her famous sarcasm, and I started to worry that perhaps I might have been a little bit *too* pushy and Simon would never talk to me again. I needed him, to get to Matt! But Monday morning he was waiting for me at the station. He said he'd had a word with Matt and they were both going to come. Three thousand cheers! *Definitely* an over-the-moon day!

I babbled at him that I was so glad. I said that we were desperate for more young people, "Cos otherwise, it's like some kind of geriatric convention". Simon said that he was pleased to be of help. He said it very solemnly, so that I couldn't tell whether he was teasing or being serious. A bit gushily – I have this pathetic tendency to gush when I am feeling unsure of myself – I said that if they wanted, he and Matt could stay over.

"We have oceans of room, it wouldn't be any problem."

Well, it wouldn't have been, they could easily have slept downstairs. I don't know what call Mum had to get so uptight about it.

"It would just be *nice*," she said, "to be consulted. I mean, who are these boys? I've never met them! I've never even heard of them before."

As it happened they didn't need to stay over, which I thought was a pity as it would have been ultra romantic to wake up and meet over the breakfast table, but in any case Mum couldn't say very much in view of my *rather dazzling* end-of-term report. In every single subject there was "marked improvement" or "she has made great strides" or even, glory hallelujah, "Scarlett has turned in some excellent work"!!! Now it was Mum's turn to be over-the-moon. She hugged me and said that she was "so pleased". Dad said, "Blimey O'Reilly, I'm living with a couple of bluestockings!" Mum told him not to tease.

"She's done so well!"

Dad winked at me and said, "Go on, it'll never last! I give it until... when do they let you know about the founder's thing? Middle of Jan? I give it till the middle of Jan!"

"That would be cheating," said Mum. "That would be false pretences!"

Oh, dear! Mum was being so earnest about it. But I have to admit, it did give me quite a warm, cosy feeling to have a favourable report for once. And while doing homework was a real drag, it was kind of satisfying when you got good marks, so I thought that most probably I would continue even if I were lucky enough to be selected. I mean, now that I'd started, I might just as well go on. On the other hand, if I didn't get selected, after all my hard work and striving to be better – well! I would be sick as a parrot. But I didn't want to think about that right now. Matt was coming to the after-Christmas party and everything was, like, **GO.**

And then disaster hit the world. This is what I wrote in my diary:

The most terrible thing. A huge tidal wave called a tsunami has killed thousands of people in Thailand. It was on the television, we were all so shocked. Mum and me were in tears, thinking of all the children that had lost their parents, and the parents who could do nothing while their children were washed away from them. Mum said, "That would be my worst nightmare," and Dad agreed with her. How can God let such things happen???

This was a question I put to Hattie, hoping she would have something comforting to say, or maybe even some kind of explanation, but Hattie just grimly stated that "There isn't any God". She said, "You know I don't believe in all that sort of thing ... big daddy god father looking after us all. It's just a fairy tale!"

*Not* very comforting; but I felt that she was probably right: there wasn't anyone up there, caring for us. Or if there was, He wasn't making a very good job of it. I don't mean to sound blasphemous, but that is the way that I saw it. I think that I still do. It is one thing if human beings behave badly and do horrible things, because we have free will and it is up to us how we use it; but there is nothing we can do to stop earthquakes and volcanoes and such, and if God can stop them and doesn't, then He is not very loving. And if He *can't* stop them, then He is not as powerful as He is supposed to be. That is all I am saying.

But there was something else which troubled me, apart from the question of God. When so many people were suffering, how could I still be excited at the thought of Matt coming to Dad's get-together? How could I still be dithering about what to wear?

I knew if I asked Dad he'd tell me not to bother my pretty little head, cos Dad really doesn't like to think about bad things. Quite often, when the news is on, he'll go and make a cup of tea or pick up a magazine. Mum says he's a bit of an ostrich like that. On the other hand, if I were to ask Mum I'd be scared she might start… not lecturing me, exactly, but going on. That is what me and Dad used to call it when Mum got on her high horse:

*going on.* In this case, going on about my obsession with clothes and the way I looked. I could do without that! So, as usual, I turned to Hattie. Hattie can always be relied upon to speak her mind, but she doesn't lecture, and she doesn't *go on.* I asked her if she thought that I was vain and shallow-minded, and Hattie gave one of her guffaws and said, "Of course you're vain! You're one of the vainest people I know." She then added that she'd probably be vain herself if she looked like me. "It's all part of the package."

Well! That solaced me *slightly.* "But what about shallow-minded?" I said.

Hattie thought about it, then went, "Mm… I s'ppose you are a bit. But no more than most people." She said that with so many truly ghastly things happening in the world, what with AIDS, and people starving, and wars and floods and hideous disasters, you couldn't afford to let it take over your life or you would most likely end up going into a deep depression or even killing yourself.

I was relieved when Hattie said this. I said, "So you reckon it's OK for me to forget about the tsunami for just a few hours?"

Hattie said, "Yes, absolutely! But I think probably we should think about it afterwards… I mean, like, maybe we should actually *do* something?"

I agreed, eagerly. "Yes! Let's do something. We could have a fundraiser!"

I was just so grateful to have been given permission to be shallow and self-centred for just the one evening.

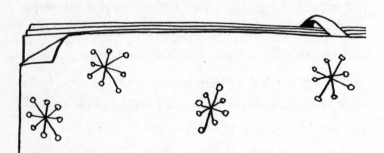

Brilliant best party of all time. Simon and the Sun God came. The Sun God — Matt! — is even more gorgeous close-up than from a distance. Sun God is the right name for him! We sat by ourselves for a while and talked, and got on really well. So well, in fact, that I plucked up my courage and asked him the question... if I am selected for Founder's Day, would he like to come with me as my partner? Looking back, I don't know how I dared! It just, like, shot out of me

before I realised what I was doing.
But it's all right, cos he has said
yes. HE HAS SAID YES! I can
hardly believe it. Just wait till I
tell Hattie!

It *was* a good party, but only because Matt was there. If he hadn't come, it would have been the same as every year: a load of grown-ups and just me and Hattie, with a couple of younger kids plus Weedy Gonzalez and my cousin Tina. Tina's OK, but she's what I would call a bit of a dimbo, meaning that she giggles a lot about nothing, and squeaks and clasps her hands together, and even presses them to her bosom (what little there is of it). Weed is a boy in my class at school. His dad and my dad play golf together and are what is known as buddies. Poor old Weed! He is terrifically geeky and boring. I know he can't help it, he is really quite nice and totally harmless, but just not anyone that I could fancy in a billion trillion years.

The best part of the evening was when we went in the pool. Me and Matt, that is. Tina and the Weed insisted on coming, too, but fortunately they can't swim so they just pottered about at the shallow end and left us pretty well in peace. Simon said no thanks and Hattie

told me, in a whisper, that she had her period, which wasn't strictly true as I knew for a fact that it had finished. Me and Hattie always know these things about each other. But I didn't say anything as I didn't want to embarrass her. She'd become very strange and oversensitive about herself just lately, and I guessed she didn't want to be seen by Matt in her bathing costume, so I told her to keep Simon amused and that we would be back in a few minutes.

In fact we stayed in the pool – or at any rate, sitting on the side of it, dangling our legs – for almost an hour. Matt said he'd never been in an indoor pool before, not in someone's actual house, so I explained how Dad was a builder and had got the place cheap and done it up.

"It was all falling to pieces... dry rot and everything."

Matt said he guessed that was one of the advantages of having a dad who did something useful. I asked him what his dad did, and he said he was a lawyer; and he pulled a face, like he didn't rate lawyers too highly in the overall scheme of things. I didn't quite know what to say to that, so for a few minutes I didn't say anything, and neither did he, and we had one of those awkward silences which always embarrass me most horribly. Then I had a moment of inspiration and asked him why Simon didn't swim.

"Is it because of his leg?"

Matt said that it was. He said, "It's not that he *can't* swim. He's just oversensitive. Thinks people will stare at him, or something."

I said, "Like Hattie!"

"Like anyone cares," said Matt.

I asked him what was wrong with Simon's leg, and he told me that he had been in the car with his dad when his dad had lost control and driven into a tree at 90 mph.

"He was in hospital for months. He's still got to have more operations."

I said, "God, if my dad did that to me he'd never forgive himself!"

Matt said he didn't know about Simon's dad forgiving himself, but Simon's mum had certainly never forgiven him.

"They've practically come apart at the seams over it."

"That is so terrible," I said. I didn't think I could bear it if my mum and dad were to come apart at the seams.

Matt said that Simon's mum was a right battle-axe. "She's another lawyer, wouldn't you know it?"

This time, it was me that pulled a face. I really don't know why I pulled one, just that it seemed to be what was expected. Lawyers, *ugh!* Women lawyers, *yuck!*

"I can't stand professional women," said Matt.

I said, "What, even though your mum is one?"

Matt said, "Yeah, even though my mum is one."

I wondered if that meant he didn't get on too well with his mum, but I didn't like to ask in case it seemed like prying. And I didn't like to ask what it was, exactly, that he had against professional women in case he thought that I approved of them, or worse still was aiming to be one. Me a lawyer! No thank *you*.

He told me, anyway. "There's just something about them… so damn *bossy* all the time. Too busy trying to beat men at their own game. Know what I mean?"

I nodded eagerly. "My dad would agree with you! That's what he thinks, too." I told him how Mum had recently got this bee in her bonnet about not having had enough education.

"And she's taking it out on me! Like I've got to work *really* hard and pass *all* these exams to make up for her not passing a single one."

"Gross," said Matt.

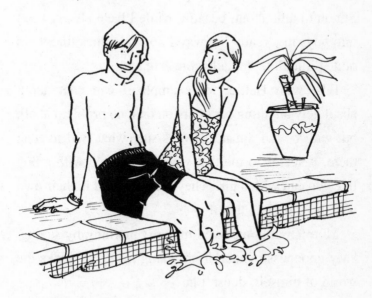

"Actually" – this was where I started to get bold – "I am sort of working a bit harder than usual, but it's nothing to do with Mum. It's because I'm trying to get selected for Founder's Day."

Matt said, "Yeah, I've heard of that. It's quite a big do, isn't it?"

So that was when I got *really* bold and asked him if he'd like to come with me as my partner, and he said that he would, and I was, like, over-the-moon!

It had been good having Simon to talk about, because while I have always been into boys in a really big way I do sometimes find them quite difficult to actually *converse* with.

Like with Hattie, for example, I can chat about absolutely anything for hours on end, no problem at all, but with boys I am not always sure what will interest them. It seems to me that you can't *gossip* with a boy like you can with a girl. They are quite odd in their own way, but I do like them!

Mum slightly annoyed me next morning by saying, "My goodness, what a flash young man! He thinks the world of himself, doesn't he?"

I asked her how she could possibly know, since as far as I was aware she hadn't even spoken to him, apart from just saying hello. Mum said, "I didn't need to speak to him, I could tell just by looking."

I said, "Well! Talk about judging people by their appearances. You are just *so prejudiced*. I suppose if he'd been black, you'd have said he was a mugger. Or if he'd had a ring in his ear, you'd have said he was on drugs. Or—"

Mum said, "Scarlett, don't be silly. You know better than that."

I thought, well, but really! Just because Matt was good looking, was that any reason to take against him? Mum really could be quite impossible, at times. I complained to Dad about it. I said, "What does she want? Would she rather I went out with some geeky little nerd?" I knew Dad wouldn't agree, cos last term when I'd gone out for a short while with Jason Francis he'd said we made a handsome couple. (Just a pity Jason was such a gunk.) "I mean, what is her *problem*?" I said.

Dad told me not to pay too much attention. "Your mum's going through a funny phase at the moment. Taking life a bit too seriously. Don't worry! She'll come through it."

I said that I hoped she would cos I was beginning to find all this constant criticism quite tiresome. Dad said, "Tell me about it!"

"I mean, what is *wrong* with her?" I said.

"Nothing," said Dad. "It'll pass."

For just a moment, when he said that, I thought I could hear a note of doubt in his voice, like maybe he wasn't so sure, after all, about it being a phase.

"God," I said, "please don't let it be permanent!"

"I'll second that," muttered Dad.

Oh, but it couldn't be! I couldn't bear it if Mum was going to turn into some sour-faced harridan without any sense of humour. I didn't think Dad could bear it, either. And then where would we be?

I decided to put it to the back of my mind. It was between Mum and Dad; there was nothing I could do about it.

In the meantime, me and Hattie didn't forget our vow to have a fundraiser for the tsunami victims. We spoke to one or two of our special friends at school and they all agreed that it was a good idea. Most of our mums and dads had made donations, but we wanted to do something by ourselves, to show that we cared. It was just a question of what. Hattie said we should call the whole of our class together after school to talk about it,

so we got permission to use the small hall and almost everyone came along. Even the boys! I say that as usually they would turn their nose up at anything organised by girls, plus they do have this tendency to mess around all the time and make stupid jokes. Fortunately Hattie was there to keep them in order. They are quite in awe of Hattie!

I don't know whose suggestion it was that we should have a beauty contest. It certainly wasn't mine! And I don't think it was Tanya's, either. But we had a show of hands and practically every hand in the room went up.

Someone then said that we should have a "beefcake" contest for the boys, so they could strip off and show their muscles, but the only boy to put his hand up and support that one was Weedy Gonzalez – who doesn't even have any muscles! I thought that was quite brave of him, actually. He's not so bad, old Weed. The rest are such spoilsports!

One of them, Anthony Meyers, said that instead of a beefcake contest we should have a Tom Bowler. Well, that is what I thought he said. I only discovered later that in fact it is a *tombola*. Just a sort of lucky dip, really. You have all these tickets with numbers on them and people pay to pick them out. If they get a number with, like, 0 on the end, that means they've won a prize. Some of us were a bit alarmed at the thought of prizes, cos where were we going to get them from? But Ant said as it was for charity any old thing would do, just so long as it wasn't too tatty, or had bits missing, so we all agreed to go home and find stuff that we didn't want any more. I said, "And we can ask our mums and dads, as well."

Patty Stevens said that she would get her mum to bake a cake, so that we could have a "Guess the Weight of the Cake" competition, and Anita Serrano, whose dad runs a restaurant, said that she would ask her dad if we could use his downstairs banqueting hall for free, one Saturday afternoon. It was all quite exciting!

I told Mum and Dad about it when I got back from school. Mum said she thought it was an excellent idea. "Except for the beauty contest. Whose suggestion was that?"

"Not mine," I said.

"Are you sure?" said Mum.

I was indignant. "Someone *else* suggested it. Then we voted on it. What's wrong with a beauty contest, anyway?"

"Nothing," said Dad. "Just a bit of harmless fun."

He chuckled. "And of course we all know who'll win!"

"It won't be me," I said, quickly. "It'll be Tanya."

"Tanya? That one that came to your party last year? Nah!" Dad shook his head. "She's a milksop beside you."

"Frank, do you have to?" said Mum. "Your daughter is quite vain enough as it is."

I felt my cheeks fire up. Hattie had said I was vain! I said, "You don't have to get all bent out of shape over it. I already told you, it wasn't my idea."

"No, but I bet you went along with it!"

"So what? So did everyone else! And if you can win prizes for – I don't know! Writing essays, or something, I don't see why you can't win prizes for the way you look."

"Exactly," said Dad. "Where's the difference?"

"The difference," said Mum, "is that one is an achievement, the other is just an accident of birth. Beauty is only skin deep, you know! It's what's inside that counts. Who's going to judge this *beauty* contest, anyway?"

I said, "All the people that come. They'll all get to vote."

"And how is it supposed to make money?"

I hadn't quite thought that one out. I said, "I dunno… I guess people will pay to come in."

"You'd better believe it," said Dad. "I'll pay to come in, don't you worry!"

Mum clicked her tongue, impatiently. She said, "I'm fighting a losing battle, aren't I?" And she swept out of the room, leaving me and Dad to exchange rueful glances.

102

"She's doing it again," I said.

"I know, I know." Dad waved a hand, as if to say, *tell me about it*. "Women get to a certain age—"

"She's not that old!" I said.

She was only forty-two: not exactly ancient. "If she'd had me when you were first married," I said, "she'd only be thirty-two. Why did you wait so long?"

"Ah. Well." A slightly shifty look came over Dad's face. "That was, like – I guess – my fault. In a way." He gave me this guilty grin. "I didn't want her to lose her figure!"

I said, "*Dad.*"

"Well, and also I wanted to keep her all to myself … just at the beginning, you know?"

"Is that the reason you never had any more?" I said.

"Why? Would you have liked us to have more?"

I'd sometimes thought about it. Hattie had two sisters and a brother, and I had occasionally wondered if I would like to be part of a large family. But on the whole I couldn't honestly say that it bothered me. I quite enjoyed being an only child. I said this to Dad, and he said, "Well, there you go, then! I shouldn't talk to your mum about this, by the way. She – ah – she needs a bit of time to get herself sorted."

I wouldn't have dreamt of talking to Mum! Talking to Mum was the very last thing I wanted to do. I wrote about it in my diary:

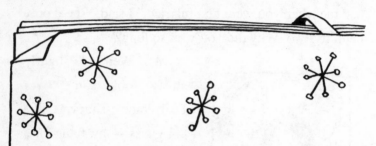

Mum is behaving so oddly these days. I just can't make her out any more. These last few months it's like she's almost become a different person. Like always NIGGLING. Always on at me not to be obsessed with the way I look, or the way other people look. Like for her looks just aren't important. But Mum has been a beauty in her time! Dad's always said that I take after her. I've seen photos of when she was young, when she and Dad were first married. The way she dressed, the way she smiled

 at the camera, like giving it the old come-on. So what's changed? Whatever it is, it's not fair on Dad! He's so proud of her, he just loves to be seen out with her. What he loves best is to be seen out with BOTH of us, me on one arm, Mum on the other. "My two girls!" I guess some people might say that was a bit yucky, but I don't see what's wrong with it. Not if it makes Dad happy. God, you'd think Mum would be flattered, after all these years, having a man that still wanted to show her off. I would be!

Mum was a puzzle, but I really didn't have time to cudgel my brains over her because all of a sudden life had become just hugely full of promise. Not just the fundraiser, not just the beauty contest, but…

Hooray hurrah and five thousand cheers! All my hard work has paid off. I HAVE BEEN SELECTED FOR FOUNDER'S DAY!!!

Hattie had been selected, too, but that came as no surprise; I'd known all along that she would be. But me!!! I could hardly believe it, even when the list was read out to us by Mr Frazer and I heard the names, Hattie Anstruther, Tanya Hoskins, Scarlett Maguire… I did this like huge sort of double take and then screamed, really loud, and clapped a hand to my mouth. I noticed

one or two people giving me these rather sour looks, like they couldn't believe it, either, and didn't think I deserved it. But I had worked *so* hard, and I hadn't been late for school once, not for the whole of last term, and I knew that my attitude was better cos lots of the teachers had remarked on it. And I wouldn't cheat and slacken off just because I'd been selected! I might relax just the tiniest little bit, but not enough to affect my grades. Whatever some people might think of me, I do have my principles and it wasn't fair of Inga Martin to go round telling everyone that it was nothing but favouritism. Just because she hadn't been selected! How could it be favouritism? I wasn't anybody's favourite! Up until the start of Year 8, I bet most of the staff thought I was a total pain. (Which I can see now that I probably was.)

Lots of people that hadn't been selected said they wouldn't have wanted to go, anyway. They said what could possibly be more boring than a stuffy old dinner and dance with teachers and governors and draggy old dignitaries from the Council. I didn't mind them saying that cos it was what I would most likely have said in their position. You have to put a brave face on things

and strictly speaking they were right, I mean there *were* going to be teachers and governors and draggy old dignitaries. But there would also be reporters and photographers, and pictures in the paper and the school magazine, not to mention, as Hattie said, the honour and glory!

Christopher Pitts, who is this huge troublemaker who would never be selected to go anywhere, unless it was in chains, actually had the nerve to suggest I should invite him as my partner. He grinned this gappy grin at me (someone had recently knocked out one of his front teeth) and said, "Go on, I dare you! Why not?"

I said, "Apart from the fact that you'd probably start chucking bread rolls at people or puking all over the place, I happen to already have a partner."

Christopher said, "Oh? Who's that, then?"

I told him it was nobody he knew. "But it's someone who won't embarrass me!" He seemed to find that amusing, for some reason. I relayed the conversation to Hattie, thinking she would agree with me that Chris Pitts was gross (though he's quite good looking, unfortunately) but Hattie just sighed and said, "I'm wondering whether I really want to come."

I said, "*What?*"

"I'm not sure," said Hattie, "I really want to come."

"Why not? What are you talking about? Of course you want to come!"

"But who can I ask to partner me?"

It came out almost in a wail. Hattie hardly ever wails. I do! I do it all the time. But Hattie is not a drama queen, and she is not as a rule self-pitying. Trying to cheer her up, I said, "You could always ask Christopher!"

"He wouldn't want to go with me," said Hattie.

"Well, he wants to go with someone!"

"No, he doesn't. He wants to go with you."

"You could ask him."

"*No!*"

"What about Weed?" I said. "He'd go with you!"

Like, *Weed would go with anyone. Weed's not fussy. He can't afford to be.* The minute I'd said it, I could have bitten my tongue out. I felt so ashamed! Hattie had turned scarlet.

"Weed's OK!" I said, quickly. "He's not nearly as geeky as he looks. He's not really geeky at *all*. You shouldn't judge people by appearances. I mean… he's actually quite a nice boy! He's far nicer than Chris. Chris is just a thug, but Weed – well, what I mean is, I wouldn't mind going with him. If I hadn't already asked Matt. And I know he likes you!"

Hattie let me burble myself to a standstill. "I'll think about it," she said. "There's no rush, it's not happening till half term."

"But you will come," I said. "Promise me you'll come!"

"I'll think about it," said Hattie.

"Yes," I said, "and I'll think, too… I'll think of someone you can ask to go with you!"

I meant to think, I really did, but there were just so many other thoughts swarming about in my brain that the problem of Hattie got crowded out. Life was just too exciting! I'd been selected for Founder's Day, Matt was coming with me,  and on Saturday we were raising money for the tsunami victims – and having our beauty contest. And Matt was coming to that, as well! I'd asked him, and he'd said that he would; him and Simon. I was so looking forward to it all! But you just never know when fate is going to strike you down.

111

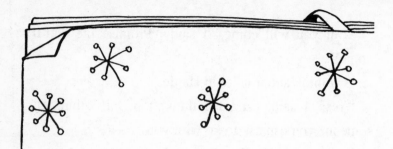

This has been the worst day in the entire history of my life. When I woke up this morning I found my face had gone all bloated and ugly, I mean like REALLY ugly, like totally grotesque. Like something out of a nightmare. I nearly died. I am not exaggerating! I couldn't bear to look at myself. It was so bad I had to miss out on the fundraiser. I am just totally GUTTED. I'd been looking forward to it for such ages! Why did it have to happen NOW???

I am living in terror in case it happens again. What is so frightening is that I don't know why it happened in the first place. Mum says it's an allergy, but to what? SHE says to make-up, but I haven't

used any make-up. Not for days!
Mum only says that cos it's the
easiest thing to pick on. It's all part
of having a go at me. Part of her
"you're too obsessed with the way
you look" thing.

But I am not obsessed! It's
perfectly normal for someone to
care about the way they look. Mum
might have got old and past it, but I
am still young, and I think she
should remember that.

My next diary entry was the last one I made for a while. All it said was, *If this goes on, then there will be no point in living. I might as well kill myself.*

I don't think I really, seriously meant it – although maybe I did, which is rather frightening. But it truly was like the end of the world. How could I ever face anyone again?

How it started: I'd gone to bed on Friday evening feeling all happy and buzzy. I'd washed my hair ready for the beauty contest, and I'd cleaned my face *so* carefully, doing all the right things, like they tell you in the magazines; and then when I woke up on Saturday morning … I couldn't believe it! I looked in the mirror and I just nearly died. *My eyes were all swollen like footballs.* I let out this piercing screech and went hurtling down the stairs shrieking, "*Mu-u-u-m!*" Mum shot out of the kitchen going, "What is it? What is it?"

"My eyes!" I bawled. "Look at my eyes!"

Mum looked. "Oh, dear, yes, they are a bit puffy, aren't they?" she said.

A *bit*??? Dad came rushing in at that point, wanting to know what all the noise was about.

"It's all right," said Mum. "Just a minor crisis."

By now I was practically in hysterics. I screamed at Mum that it wasn't minor. "I'm supposed to be going in for a beauty contest! How can I even *show* myself?"

Dad took a look and said, "She's right, she can't go in for any beauty contest in that state."

Dad's reaction only made me even more hysterical. Mum told me to calm down.

"It's nowhere near as bad as you make out. Eat your breakfast, then go upstairs and lie down for an hour and you'll probably find you're back to normal."

"But what can be causing it?" said Dad.

"Anything," said Mum. "She's obviously like me; she's got sensitive skin." Mum said it was the price we paid for being redheads. She tried to make me eat something but I couldn't; I just wanted to get upstairs, in a darkened room, and go to sleep, so that I could wake up and be my usual self. Mum gave me some cotton wool pads soaked in witch hazel to put on my eyes. I wanted to use a proper soothing lotion, but Mum told me sharply to "Forget all that proprietary stuff! It's just junk. Witch hazel's far better for you. Now lie down and try to relax."

I did try, but it wasn't easy. Every few minutes I kept touching at my eyes, checking whether they were still puffy and then getting in a panic cos I'd think they were getting worse, which meant grabbing a mirror and switching on the bedside lamp to inspect myself.

Mum came in at half-past eleven and said, "Well, how's it going? Let me have a look… oh, that's much better! It hardly even notices."

But it still *did* notice. I sobbed that I couldn't go in for a beauty contest with eyes that were all wrinkled and red. Dad agreed with me. I pleaded with Mum to ring Hattie and tell her I'd got the flu. Mum said, "Oh, now, come on, Scarlett! That's a bit over the top. You can still go, just miss out on the beauty bit."

I shouted, "I'm not going anywhere like this!"

Dad said he could understand how I felt. He told Mum that she would have been just the same when she was my age and Mum had to admit that he was probably right.

"I was pretty vain in those days, wasn't I?"

"You had a lot to be vain about," said Dad. "It's almost worse for a pretty girl to lose her looks than a plain one. Not that she has lost her looks," he added hastily, before I could set off screaming again. "It's nowhere near as bad as it was."

"But will you please, *please* tell Hattie I've got the flu?" I begged. I didn't want people knowing the state I was in. I especially didn't want Matt knowing. Lying in bed with a high temperature might be thought at least a little bit romantic, but having eyes embedded in elephant skin was just gross.

By six o'clock, when Hattie rang back to see how I was, the elephant skin had virtually disappeared. Even I had to peer at myself in the magnifying side of Dad's shaving mirror to see the last lingering traces of it, which meant I'd stopped worrying about how I was ever going to be able to go out again without dark glasses and instead was full of bitter frustration at having missed the fundraiser.

"It's so annoying," I said. "I want to hear all about it! Was Matt there?"

Hattie said yes, he was. "I told him you'd got the flu. You're obviously feeling loads better. Are you sure it's the flu? Lots of people say they've got flu when really all they've got is a cold. Colds are quite different! Flu can be serious. If you'd actually got the flu you'd still be feeling ghastly."

I said, "I am still feeling ghastly and if you don't stop wittering and get on with things I'll start feeling even more ghastly!"

"Oh. All right," said Hattie. "What do you want to know?"

"*Who won the beauty contest?*"

Hattie said, "Give you three guesses!"

I didn't need three guesses. Glumly I said, "Tanya?"

Without me, who else was there? In spite of what I'd said to Dad, about Tanya probably winning, I'd secretly believed that it would be me. It wasn't vanity! Well, maybe it was vanity that I'd so desperately *wanted* it to be me and maybe it was vanity that I was now so jealous of Tanya, but I didn't see how it could be vanity to know that I was pretty. Dad had been telling me that I was almost ever since I could remember.

"Did you vote for her?" I said.

"I didn't vote for anyone," said Hattie. "I decided in the end it was a bit demeaning... like Best in Show for dogs." She added that she thought that was demeaning, as well, but I wasn't particularly interested just then in Hattie and her dotty opinions. I sometimes think that she and Mum would make a good pair. It's odd, because Hattie's mum is quite normal.

"I wonder who Matt voted for?" I said.

"Haven't the faintest idea," said Hattie. "Why not ask him when he rings you?"

Eagerly I said, "Is he going to?"

"So he says. Said he'd give you a call tomorrow to see how you were."

Well! That cheered me up hugely. By the time I went to bed I was feeling almost happy again, especially as my eyes were practically back to normal. I cleaned my face even *more* carefully than I had the previous night 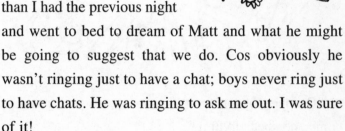 and went to bed to dream of Matt and what he might be going to suggest that we do. Cos obviously he wasn't ringing just to have a chat; boys never ring just to have chats. He was ringing to ask me out. I was sure of it!

And then I woke next morning and my eyes were swollen worse than ever.

It was the beginning of the nightmare. As I look back, it all seems to merge into one block of horror. These are just a few of the things that I remember.

Lying in bed, on Sunday afternoon, with the curtains closed and witch hazel pads over my eyes. There's a knock at the door, and Mum comes in.

"Scarlett?" she says. "Your flash young man has called. Do you want to come down?"

"*Come down?*" I tear off the witch hazel pads and stare at Mum in horror. "You mean he's actually *here*?"

"Dropped by on the off chance. Are you going to come and speak to him?"

Is Mum mad? Does she really think I'm going to show myself to Matt in this state?

"Come on," she says, "be brave! You can put my sunglasses on."

"*No!*" Why would I be wearing sunglasses when I was supposed to have the flu? "Tell him I'm ill! Tell him to phone me!"

"Oh, all right," says Mum.

The minute she's gone I leap out of bed and race to the door. By opening it just a crack I can hear Mum, down in the hall, talking to Matt.

"...some kind of allergy. Her face is a bit swollen. It's not as bad as she makes out, but you know Scarlett... won't be seen dead unless she's blemish-free and perfect."

How could she? *How could she?* I hurl myself back on to my bed and scream silently into the pillow. When I accuse Mum, later, of betraying me, she says she's sorry, she'd forgotten it was the flu.

"Just stop overreacting," she says. "I know it's not very nice, but it's not as if it's life-threatening. If you'd just stop looking at yourself in the mirror every five minutes, you might find it went away."

I sob and say that she obviously thinks I'm some kind of neurotic.

"I think you'll turn yourself into one," says Mum, "if you don't relax a bit."

I yell that I am relaxing. "I'm lying here with these stupid bits of cotton wool soaked in stupid witch hazel and they're not doing the least bit of good!"

To which all Mum can think to say in reply is, "In that case, why don't you come downstairs and join us for tea? You can always put the glasses on," she says, "if you'd rather Dad didn't see you."

So I put the glasses on and they're the cheap kind that make everything just like totally pitch black, so I have to keep lifting them up to find out where things are.

Mum says maybe she should make me a veil, out of curtain netting. I immediately burst into tears and have to be comforted by Dad, who reprovingly tells Mum that "This is no joking matter!" Mum agrees that it isn't, but says I am grossly overplaying it and nobody who didn't actually know me would ever realise there was anything wrong. Dad says that is not the point.

"There is something wrong and she's naturally upset. If she's like this tomorrow, she'll have to see the doctor."

That's my second memory: seeing the doctor. Cos when I wake up on Monday morning I'm, like, right back to square one, huge great puffballs where my eyes are supposed to be. You can hardly even see my eyes, they're so swollen. I scream hysterically at Mum that *no way* am I going in to school to be laughed at. Dad says there's no question of my going in to school.

"You're going straight to the doctor!"

Well, you can't go *straight* to the doctor (not unless you're dying, and maybe not even then) cos you have to make an appointment, and the first free slot is days away. It's not until Dad's angrily snatched the telephone from Mum and bellowed into it that the dragon woman who guards the entrance to the cave grudgingly says I can come along at six o'clock that evening. So I spend another day lying on my bed, and by the time I finally get to the surgery with Mum my eyes have, like, subsided a bit, only now the elephant skin is back. It looks like the skin of some ancient old crone.

The doctor is a complete idiot. He says, "Hello, it's Scarlett, isn't it? And what's wrong with Scarlett this fine day?"

I say, "*This*," and whip off my glasses.

He looks at me and says, "So what's the problem? You look very pretty!"

I scream that my eyes are all puffed up.

He says, "Are they?" and peers a bit closer.

I screech that of course they are! "You don't think they're normally like this, do you?"

He says apologetically that they might be; how should he know? He's never seen me before. Mum then steps in to explain that the swelling's gone down a bit since this morning, but it was quite bad.

"We think it's probably some kind of allergy... all the muck she puts on her face."

 I roar at her that I haven't *got* muck on my face. "I don't *put* muck on my face! Do you see any muck on my face? I haven't got *anything* on my face!"

Mum says, "Well, not right at this moment, maybe. But some of that stuff... you never know what it's got in it."

The doctor agrees with Mum. He says you can't be too careful. "Especially if you have that type of skin." He says what Mum said about being a redhead. He says, "I'm afraid beauty sometimes comes at a price." He tells me to take antihistamine tablets and on no account to put anything whatsoever on my face.

"Just let it breathe for a while."

"An excellent idea," says Mum.

She's always been anti make-up. But I haven't used any! We sit round the table that evening, me and Mum and Dad, trying to work out what else I could be allergic to, like my pillow, or house dust, or cheese, or – almost anything. Mum still says the most likely culprit is something I've put on myself. There isn't any point in arguing with her; she gets these ideas. Nothing will change them.

Hattie rings later, wanting to know how I am. I glumly inform her that I've got an allergy. She says, "Oh, horrible! Poor you," and goes on to tell me how much money we made at the fundraiser. I know it's very wrong of me, but just at this moment I don't care two straws about the fundraiser. I don't even care about the tsunami victims. All those poor people who died, or lost their loved ones. I just care about me and my face!

Later on, the phone rings again. This time it's Matt, also wanting to know how I am.

"Are you going to be presentable in time for the Founder's Day thing?"

I squawk in protest at him, down the phone. "God, I should hope so!"

Founder's Day isn't for another three weeks. I can't still be in this state in three weeks!

But I can. This is just the start of the nightmare. Next day when I wake up I grab the mirror and this thing, this loathsome, hideous, unspeakable *thing*, leers back at me, like some kind of deformed monstrosity out of a horror movie. Overnight, my entire face has swollen up. I just scream, and scream, and scream. Mum comes running, and so does Dad. Now even Mum can't say that I'm over-reacting. Dad is almost as panic-stricken as I am; he wants to rush me straight down to the A & E department. It's Mum – as always – who keeps her head. She says this is proof positive I'm allergic to something.

"Now, Scarlett, think!" she says. "And be honest… *what have you been putting on your face?*"

I sob hysterically that I haven't been putting anything on my face.

"I'm sorry, but I just don't believe you," says Mum. And she pulls open the door of my bedside cabinet and starts rooting about inside it. "Cleansing lotion! Did you use any cleansing lotion?"

"I didn't need to! I wasn't wearing any make-up."

"OK. What about eye shadow?"

"No!"

"What about mascara?"

"No!"

"Lipstick?"

"*No!*"

"What's this stuff? *Toner*? What do you want toner for, at your age? For goodness' sake! All this junk. Gel cleanser, correction stick—"

"That's for spots! I haven't used it."

"What about this? *Mattifying moisturiser?*"

"No!"

"*Soothing day cream?*"

I open my mouth – and then close it again. Mum says, "Scarlett, you didn't?"

I desperately want to say no, but I hesitate just a fraction of a second too long.

"For crying out loud!" Mum's holding up the jar, squinting at the list of contents. "*Fragrance*. It's got perfume in it!"

She unscrews the lid and takes a sniff. "That is disgusting!

128

Totally artificial. No wonder you've made such a mess of yourself! You used it last night, didn't you?"

Guiltily, I nod. It hadn't seemed to me that the witch hazel was doing anything very much, so yes, I've been using the cream.

"It said it was soothing! I thought it would be good for me!"

"Not," says Mum, "with perfume in it. Not with skin like yours."

Now I'm sobbing again. Dad's like really scared.

"It won't have done any permanent damage, will it?"

"No, but it'll probably take a while before it settles down. She'll need to get it out of her system."

Dad rises up at this, in a rage. He says if this is what the product does to people, it shouldn't be on sale. He's shouting and striding about the room and threatening to sue. And he still wants to take me to A & E. Mum stands firm. She says, "At least we've discovered what's causing it."

It's the only comfort I have, that at least now I *know*. Dad's still muttering about the hospital. He says, "We can't leave her in this state!"

In the end he lets Mum talk him out of it on the grounds that she's the expert when it comes to skin care. She's always had to be careful what she puts on her face and it looks like I'm going to be the same. Mum gives me a pot of her extra special and hugely expensive, anti-allergic skin lotion to use, and promises me that "It will clear up... just be patient."

Unfortunately, being patient is the last thing I'm any good at. I take after Dad. Mum always says that "Your dad's like a child... wants everything right now, like immediately." I am exactly the same. When Mum said it could take a week or two before my face was back to normal, I just nearly freaked. I was still waking up five or six times a night to look in the mirror and check I hadn't swollen up again. By the end of the week most of the puffiness had gone, but I was back to elephant skin. *Red* elephant skin. All rough, and lined, and wrinkly. Mum said that give it time and it would start peeling off. She said that underneath my skin would be smooth, just like it was before. I told myself that Mum knew what she was talking about, but I still couldn't help waves of terror engulfing me, specially in the middle of the night, because suppose Mum *didn't* know? Suppose she was wrong? *Suppose I was always going to be like this?*

Hattie rang to check my progress and to ask if she should come round, but I said not yet. I didn't even want Hattie seeing me with elephant skin. Matt rang, too, and I told him I was getting better. I assured him I would be all right for Founder's Day, cos I didn't want him giving up on me and arranging to go and do something else. Especially not with another girl.

Jokingly he said that he would "Send Si round to check… unless I'm allowed to come and check for myself?"

I wanted to scream *"NO!"* at the top of my voice, but forced myself, instead, to giggle and say, "Well, if you're into horror movies!"

"Bad as that?" said Matt.

It is actually not funny, having to tell a boy you fancy like crazy that you look like something in a pickle jar, but it was either that or bursting into tears and I just had this feeling Matt was not the sort of guy who could deal with tears.

On Friday in the local paper there was a report of our fundraiser, with a big syrupy picture of Tanya being crowned beauty queen.

"Not a patch on you," said Dad.

"Oh, never mind that!" said Mum. "How about all this money they've raised? Scarlett, it's wonderful! Don't you think so?"

I said that I did, to keep Mum happy, but really it didn't mean anything. I told myself that I was now being *truly* shallow, worrying about the way I looked when there were poor little children who had lost their mums and dads, and mums and dads frantic with grief cos of having lost their children. I mean, I did *try* to put things in perspective, I really, really did. I felt so ashamed of myself! But every time I looked in the mirror it just seemed like totally unimportant. The only thing that seemed important was me and my face. How could I go on living like some kind of freak?

After about ten days, Mum wanted me to go back to school. I refused, point blank. I wasn't going back to school with bits of skin hanging off me!

"And look at my eyes… they're like an old person's!"

Mum said, "It's really not that bad any more. Certainly not bad enough to miss all this schooling. You've been doing so well this year! We don't want you falling behind."

I said, "What does it matter? *Really?*"

"It matters," said Mum. "Believe me!"

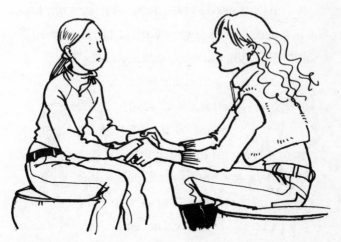

And then told me to sit down. She said, "Scarlett, we have to have a talk. There's something I've been meaning to tell you. I didn't want to do it while you were still in such a state, and I don't want you to be too

133

upset, but the fact is your dad and I have been doing a lot of soul-searching these last few weeks and we've finally come to a decision. That is... I've come to a decision. And your dad has agreed. I'm going to be moving out for a while. Just for a while! We're not getting divorced, we're not splitting up. It's not even a proper separation."

In this small, tight voice I heard myself say, "So what is it, then?"

"It's more like a – a *trial* separation. Not even that! Your dad and I haven't quarrelled, we still love each other, it's just... I need to be on my own for a bit. I need my own space. Just to get myself sorted. You know?"

I said, "No! What are you talking about?"

"I want an education," said Mum. "I want to go to college. I want to get a degree!"

I stared at her, blankly. "What for?"

Mum said it was something she just had to do. "I suppose... I don't know! I suppose I just feel the need to exercise my brain. I never used it, all the time I was

134

at school… total waste! So I'm going to enrol for classes, and see how I get on."

I said, "But why do you have to leave home?"

"It's just until I get the hang of things – or until your dad gets the hang of things. I love your dad dearly, but he's not always the most supportive. If he could just bring himself to give me a bit of encouragement… It's really quite difficult, going back to school again at my age, especially when you have to start right from square one. I can't cope with your dad putting me down all the time! I can see that it's difficult for him. I'm not the person he married! It's just one of those things… it happens. It isn't anybody's fault."

It seemed to me that it was. "You're the one that's changed!" I said.

"Yes," said Mum, "I accept that. But, Scarlett, people can't help the way they develop! I really do need to do something with my life. I mean, something of my own. You'll be off to uni before we know it, your dad's business is doing very nicely without me… I just feel the need to move on."

"You mean, move out," I said.

"No! I mean, *move on*. To the next stage. I can't just stagnate! I know your dad can't understand, and probably at this moment you can't, either, but I'm hoping that in time you both will, and then – well, then maybe I can come back and we can all get on with our lives!"

She smiled at me, like she was saying that she would just pop down to the shops for a couple of hours, then she would come back and we could all cosily have tea. Coldly, I said, "So when are you going?"

"The end of next week," said Mum. "But I won't be far away! I've got a flat in town… just one room and a kitchen. I can always put you up on the sofa if you want to stay the night."

"I don't think that's very likely," I said.

"Oh, Scarlett, please! Don't be like that," said Mum. "I know it seems like I'm being totally selfish, and maybe perhaps I am, but it's not a step I'm taking lightly. Believe me! It's not a spur of the moment decision… I've been thinking of it for a very long time."

Somehow, that just made it even worse. The thought of Mum secretly brooding to herself. Plotting and planning how she was going to leave us. Planning to walk out!

"Scarlett?" She smiled, hopefully. "Come and give me a kiss and tell me you don't hate me."

But I wouldn't. Cos I did hate her! I wrote furiously in my diary that I hated, hated, *hated* her.

She can sweet-talk as much as she likes. She needn't think she's going to get round me! I shall never forgive her for what she's doing to Dad. He loves her SO MUCH. He's always telling her how beautiful she is, and how proud he is of her. She ought to think herself lucky, having a husband like that! He's never been mean to her; not once. Mum's the one that's always nagging and finding fault. At least, just lately. She never used to be like that. We used to be a real family. We used to be HAPPY. Now she's gone and ruined it all, and I just don't know what Dad's ever done to deserve it. He's never so much as LOOKED at another woman. Lots of men do, but not my dad. Serve her right if he

> went out and got a girlfriend. Half
> her age and twice as pretty. Oh,
> God, I hate her! I hate her, I HATE
> her!

I thought that it simply wasn't true, what Mum had said. Dad didn't put her down all the time, he just pulled her leg a bit. Like when she got too serious he'd tell her to chill, or to lighten up. That wasn't putting her down! That was just teasing. It certainly didn't seem to me a good enough reason for her to walk out on us. She could just as easily have stayed put and done her stupid studying during the day, when me and Dad weren't around. Do it all night as well, if she wanted. It wouldn't worry me and Dad! We wouldn't interfere. We'd just do our own thing, same as we always did, and let her get on with it. But at least she'd have *been* here.

When I asked Dad about it, he just hunched a shoulder and said, "You know your mum. She gets these ideas."

"But what's the point of it?" I said. "What's she want a degree for? What's she going to do with it?"

"I guess it will make her feel good," said Dad. "Load of nonsense, if you ask me, but if that's what she wants…"

"But what about what *we* want?"

"Doesn't seem to matter what we want," said Dad. "She's a very wilful woman, your mother."

"She's *selfish*," I said.

"That's one way of looking at it," agreed Dad.

"I mean… what are we going to do? How are we going to manage? I can't cook!"

"Don't you worry," said Dad. "We'll survive. We'll get stuff sent in, we'll go and eat out … we'll have a whale of a time! We'll eat junk food till it comes out of our ears. While the cat's away … " He winked at me. "Make hay while the sun shines, and all that."

Dad was trying very hard to pretend he didn't care, but I knew that he did. I can always tell when Dad's putting it on. He's a very up-front kind of person, far more huggy and kissy than Mum. When he's feeling happy, he likes everyone to join in. When he's feeling

ANGRY, then, boy, the whole world has to suffer! But when something really, really gets to him, like deep down inside, he goes into what Mum used to call his "macho mode". All blokeish and blustery and couldn't give a damn. It was what he was doing now, and I just played along cos that was what seemed easiest.

"At least she won't be able to keep nagging at me," I said. "Like passing exams is the only thing that gives you any right to even *exist*."

"I never passed an exam in my life," said Dad.

"She's so hung up about it! It's just, like, nag nag nag, the whole time."

"Not any more," said Dad. "You just do your own thing. There'll be no nagging from now on."

I'd almost made up my mind that that was it: I was through with working my brains to a frazzle. Knocking myself out to pass stupid exams! Who needed them? Like Dad said, he had never passed one in his life and look at the business he'd built up, look at the house we lived in. Not a single other person in my class had a house with an indoor pool! Hattie's mum and dad were both teachers, so they'd obviously passed exams, but you could have put their poky little place in our back garden and still have room for a tennis court or two. Mum was talking total rubbish!

I think that not doing any more homework was my way of getting at her. She'd been so pleased and proud when I'd had a good report. Now I'd get a bad one, a real stinker, and that would really hurt her. After all, she was hurting me, why shouldn't I hurt her back?

But then Hattie called round, lugging books and homework assignments. She said, "Why aren't you at school? You look perfectly normal!"

"Well, I'm not," I said. "Why do you think I'm wearing sunglasses?"

"Mm…" Hattie put her head on one side, pretending to think about it. "Don't want to be recognised?"

I said, "Ha ha, very funny. Why have you brought all this stuff?"

"Mrs Wymark asked me."

"What for?"

"So you can keep up with things. She said that you've become one of her star pupils. She said it would be a terrible shame if you got left behind."

I said, "Huh!" trying to disguise the fact that I was secretly thrilled to bits to think I was becoming anyone's star pupil. I didn't *want* to be thrilled, but I just couldn't help it. Me! A star pupil! "Did she really say that?" I said. "You're not just making it up?"

"I'm not making it up," said Hattie. "She was going to come round herself if I couldn't manage it."

So that was the end of my cunning plan to get back at Mum, cos after Hattie had gone I sat down and looked at the various assignments. Before I knew it I'd started off on one of them and, weirdly and oddly, and totally against my wishes, I found that I was quite enjoying the sensation of actually doing some work again. When I next bumped into Mum (I was trying my best to avoid her) Mum said brightly, "Did Hattie bring you your homework?" I just grunted, and shoved my way past. I was no longer on speaking terms with Mum.

The day after Hattie called with my homework, Simon came. I saw him from my bedroom window and immediately grabbed my glasses, but it was several minutes before Mum called up the stairs.

"Scarlett, it's Simon. Are you going to come down?"

I stuck my head over the banisters and yelled, "Tell him to come up!"

"Oh. All right," said Mum. She sounded surprised, but I didn't want to be downstairs talking to Simon with Mum hovering around. Mum was definitely *not* my favourite person.

Me and Simon sat in my room, with me on the floor and Simon on the bed, and he explained how Matt had sent him "To check how you're getting on."

"What, and then report back?" I said.

Simon grinned and said, "You've got it! He wants to know whether he's still going to partner you on Founder's Day."

I said, "Yes!" I thought it was so strange, the way things worked out. I was remembering how Hattie's nickname for Simon had been "Hermes, messenger of the gods." And here he was, running errands for the Sun God! It was like Hattie was some kind of prophet. "Tell him I'm heaps better," I said.

"But your mum says you won't go back to school."

I said, "Oh, well! *My mum.*"

"I think she's nice," said Simon.

I said, "Huh! You might." I obviously sounded bitter, cos he asked me what the matter was.

"Aren't you getting along?"

I said, "She's leaving home!"

I don't know why I blurted it out to Simon when I hadn't even told Hattie. I mean, I tell Hattie *everything*. But Simon sounded genuinely concerned; and maybe, too, I was thinking of what Matt had told me, about Simon's mum and dad almost coming apart at the seams after his dad had crashed the car. It made me feel that he would be sympathetic. He would be able to understand in a way that Hattie couldn't, cos Hattie's mum and dad are like really close. Hattie would feel sorry for me, but it wasn't like anything she had ever experienced.

We had this long talk, me and Simon, all about parents and what it did to their kids when they fell out. Simon said that his mum and dad still weren't properly speaking to each other, and that sometimes his dad went off for days and didn't tell them where he was going. He said, "It's like living in a war zone. I almost wish they'd part company and get it over with."

"You mean, like, get divorced?" I said.

Simon said anything would be better than how it was at the moment. I said, "I couldn't bear if it my mum and dad got divorced!"

"You still love your mum, don't you?" said Simon.

I said, "No! I hate her!" And then I went and burst into tears and had to get a tissue and try to mop up under cover of my glasses.

"Did she say why she's leaving?"

I told him that it was purely selfish and that she just wanted to exercise her brain. "She wants to get a *degree*. At her age!"

"Better late than never," said Simon. "Lots of older people go and get degrees."

"But what does she want it for? It's stupid! She won't do anything with it when she's got it."

"How do you know?" said Simon. "She might want to go off and be a teacher, or a – lawyer, or something."

"That's what your mum is, isn't it?" I said. "Do you mind having a mum that works?"

"Mind?" He seemed puzzled. "Why should I mind?"

"I don't know! It just seems nicer if you have a mum that stays home and looks after you."

"She did when we were little. She wouldn't want to now; she'd get bored. That's probably what's happened to your mum. I mean… what does she do all day?"

I thought about it. What did Mum do all day? "She used to help my dad," I said. "But he doesn't need it now, he can afford to employ people."

146

"Well, there you go," said Simon.

He seemed to be on Mum's side! He said, "It's a pity she has to go off and be by herself, but … "

"She says she needs to get sorted. She says *Dad* needs to get sorted. Dad's never passed an exam in his life, he doesn't see any need for it."

Carefully, Simon said, "Well, your dad's obviously done all right, but maybe now your mum wants to, as well."

"You mean, like… do her own thing?"

"I'd want to," said Simon, "wouldn't you? Or are you going to be one of those women that just lives in their partner's shadow?"

"Now you're sounding like Hattie!" I said. "She's the hugest feminist."

I expected him to pull a face, cos most boys, in my experience, don't much go for feminist type women. Hattie says that secretly they are afraid of them. She says they feel threatened. On the other hand, Matt had pulled a face and I could hardly believe that Matt felt threatened.

Dad pulled faces, too, but I wasn't so sure about Dad.

"Hattie's really militant," I said. "She won't live in anyone's shadow. She'll most likely end up as prime minister."

"Good for her," said Simon.

"I don't know whether she'll ever find a man," I said. "I mean… I don't even know whether she'd *want* to find a man." I added this last bit rather quickly, in case Simon thought I was casting aspersions. Implying that Hattie wasn't attractive enough to find one. It wasn't what I'd meant! All I'd meant was that being so terrifically feminist, and so tremendously *focused*, she might prefer to concentrate on just having a career.

I explained this to Simon. He said, "Well, that's OK, if that's her choice. Nothing wrong with it. But there's no reason she shouldn't have both; lots of people do."

We sat talking for simply ages. It was really interesting; I'd never been able to talk like that with a boy before. It was almost as good as talking to Hattie! I felt I could say anything, and he would take it seriously. Most boys (the ones I've met) don't seem to like talking about people, or about feelings, or even just ordinary everyday life. They're either very stiff and awkward, like girls are some kind of alien life form they've never met before, or they turn everything into a joke, and say things to make you blush. Matt was a bit like that. I remembered when we'd sat by the pool after Christmas. Once we'd exhausted the subject of Simon and his mum and dad, Matt had started joshing around, being flirty

148

and trying to make me blush. But that was OK, because that was Matt. I certainly wouldn't want Simon to be that way! But I have to say it did make a nice change, being able to sit and talk instead of feeling all the time that I had to be girly.

When Simon had left, Mum said, "Well, he seems like a sensible young man. A bit more to him than there is to Flash Harry!" I thought, God, Mum is *so* predictable.

After that, Simon took to calling by most days on his way back from school. Officially he came to drop off my homework assignments and collect what I'd already done. It was easier for him than for Hattie, because Hattie lived way over the other side of town. She said they'd arranged to meet at the station every morning, as they got off their trains, and do an exchange: old for new.

"Like a couple of spies!" she giggled, over the telephone.

When Mum learnt that Simon went home to an empty house every afternoon she insisted that he stay and have tea. She said, "It's all right, you can have it by yourselves, I won't interfere." I was glad Mum left us alone, because we just had so many things to talk about – including Mum herself. She was going off any day now to start living in her rented cube, as she called it, and although I kept up a cold front of hostility, I was actually quite frightened. How could she do this to us? How were we going to survive? In all my twelve years, Mum had never been away from home even just for one night! I'd told Hattie by now, thinking she would be as shocked and horrified as I was, but Hattie said she could understand why Mum felt she had to get away for a bit. She said, "I like your dad, but he is a bit, sort of… stifling."

I didn't think Hattie had any right to say that about my dad. It didn't help! But talking to Simon made me feel a bit less scared and a bit more hopeful. He said he didn't think I should shut Mum out.

"I know she's the one that's doing it to you, but she's probably feeling quite gutted, too. And you do want her back again, don't you?"

I said, "Yes, I do! I don't want her to go in the first place!"

"I think you ought to tell her," said Simon. "At least she'll know you still love her."

"She already knows that!" I said.

"Yeah, well, OK, maybe, but it wouldn't hurt to tell her."

I couldn't; I still couldn't bring myself even to talk to Mum, let alone tell her that I loved her. Dad wasn't saying much, either, so life at home was really pretty miserable. And I was *still* hiding behind sunglasses. It was Hattie who nagged me, now, not Mum.

"When are you coming back to school? You'll have to come back some time! You can't still be looking like something out of a horror movie?"

I said, "No, I just look like a pickled walnut!" My eyes were still crinkled and I still had dry patches on my face. I wasn't going back to school in that state!

"Well, it's up to you," said Hattie. "But you're going to find it really difficult, making up for lost time."

*So what?* I would go back when I was good and ready, and not before. Hattie had no right to bully me! Friends weren't supposed to bully each other. And then, wouldn't you know it? Simon started on at me! He said, "Tell me, how much longer are you going to go on behaving like a leper?"

I snapped, "Until I've stopped looking like one! I look like a pickled walnut!"

"I don't believe you," said Simon.

I said, "Oh, really? And how would you know? You haven't got the faintest idea *what* I look like if I take these glasses off!"

That was a mistake, cos he immediately said, "Well, go on, then! Do it! Then I can see."

"I don't want you to see! I don't want anyone to see!"

"Your mum's seen. She says you're just making a fuss about nothing."

"Yeah, well, she would, wouldn't she? She just wants to *pretend* that I'm OK so she can go waltzing off and not have pangs of conscience!"

"What about Matt?" said Simon. "He's getting worried. There's only a couple of weeks to go to

Founder's Day and he still doesn't know whether he's going to partner you or not. I'm supposed to be reporting back! He's nagging me to know if you're presentable. What am I going to tell him? She's still in hiding and won't let anyone see her?"

I said, "Now you're trying to blackmail me."

He didn't deny it. But sort of apologetically he said, "You know what Matt's like."

I said, "What d'you mean?"

"Well—" He shrugged.

"What do you mean? *Know what Matt's like?*"

So then Simon looked a bit uncomfortable and mumbled, "If you're not going to be able to go, he'll probably go with someone else."

"Someone else?" I felt my heart began to hammer in my rib cage. "Who?"

"I don't know who."

"Has someone else asked him?"

"I dunno! Well – yeah. I think so. I'm not sure. He just told me to check you're going to be OK."

"I am going to be OK!"

"So what do I say when he asks me if I've – like – well! Seen you," said Simon.

There was a silence. My heart was still hammering. Who was it who had *dared* ask my date to go with her to Founder's Day? Instead of me! Who else did Matt know?

"Thing is," said Simon, "he's used to, like, having his pick. Been spoilt, I guess."

Well, and so had I; I was used to having *my* pick. But I would just die if Matt were to go to Founder's Day with someone else!

"Be brave," said Simon. "Just take them off... I'll tell you if you look like a pickled walnut. Honest! Give you my word. If I say you don't, you can trust me... you don't!"

I took a breath, trying to stop my heart going at it like a bongo drum. Slowly I said, "All right... I'll make a bargain with you. I'll take my glasses off if you'll come in the pool."

Oh! That was different. He didn't like it when I turned the tables on him.

"I told you," he muttered, "I don't swim."

"Matt said you did. He said you *could*. He said you just wouldn't, cos of being scared people would stare. That's as pathetic as me not taking my glasses off. It's just vanity. Like anybody *cares* how you look. Actually, it's worse for me cos Matt *does* care how I look. So if I'm going to be brave then you ought, too!"

"But I haven't got any bathing trunks."

154

"No problem! We've got loads, we keep them specially. You won't get out of it that way!"

He agreed, in the end. I could tell he wasn't happy, but I stood firm. He was being mean to me, I would be mean to him! It wasn't till I'd changed into my swimsuit – in my bedroom – and taken off my glasses and studied myself up close in the mirror, that I started to feel a bit guilty. I really *didn't* look too bad. I almost began to feel ashamed of all the fuss I'd been making. It had been horrendous at the beginning, but Mum was right: I could have gone back to school days ago.

I went racing downstairs and into the pool room, and banged on the door of the changing cubicle.

"Hey, Simon!"

"I'm coming," he said.

"No, I wanted to tell you, it's OK, you don't have to, I'm sorry! I've taken my glasses off, you can look, but I won't make you undress. You don't have to go in the pool!"

"Actually," he said, "I do." He opened the door of the cubicle and I tried very hard not to stare at his leg, cos a) it would have been rude, not to mention insensitive, and b) it would have embarrassed him; but quite calmly he said, "It's all right, I've psyched myself up for it. I should have done it before. It's just stupid vanity."

"Me, too," I said.

Simon said no, I was right, it was worse for me. He said, "I guess it's always worse for girls." I told him very firmly that he was being sexist – though in the nicest possible way – and that it was in fact worse for him, because my eyes had only

156

swollen up through my own stupidity, whereas he couldn't help what had happened to him.

"Plus I'm almost back to normal, but Matt said you'd got to have more operations?"

Simon said, "Yeah, well… that's the way it goes. And you *are* back to normal. You don't look in the least like a pickled walnut!"

"So will you tell Matt?" I said.

He promised that he would, and we both went into the pool and sploshed up and down for a bit, then sat on the side and talked. We were there for ages! Simon was such an easy person to talk to. He told me more about his mum and dad, and how they'd got on really well before his dad had gone and trashed the car. And then he thought about it and said maybe that wasn't quite true; maybe they *hadn't* got on quite so well. The reason his dad had trashed the car was that he was in a towering great rage.

"He and my mum had just had this really big fight and Dad was, like, still seething. So I guess, maybe, him screwing up just brought matters to a head. It's funny," he said, "I've never really admitted that before. I've always liked to believe that everything was perfect. But looking back, I can see that it wasn't. Not really. There were all sorts of clues."

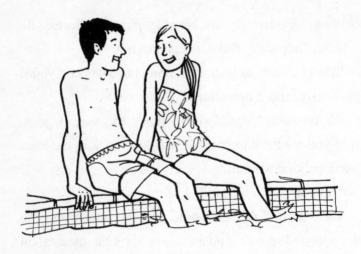

I said that when *I* looked back, I couldn't see any clues at all.

"Not until these last few months." Before that, everything *had* been perfect. I said this to Simon, and he said maybe it had only seemed so.

"It could be something that's been building up for ages. Like your mum could have been feeling more and more frustrated and just, like, keeping the lid on things?"

I said doubtfully that I supposed it was possible.

"Doesn't strike me as something that'd come on suddenly," said Simon. "It might have seemed sudden, when she finally came out with it, but that's only because you didn't know what was going on."

"No," I said, "and neither did Dad!"

"You reckon?"

"I'm sure he didn't!"

"He probably did," said Simon. "People usually do. They just close their minds because they don't want to know. If you let yourself know, it means you have to do something."

"Like what?" I said. "There's not much you can do if your mum walks out!"

"Just give her a bit of time. Give them both a bit of time. I'm sure they'll work things through. Your mum seems like a really together person."

"What about my dad? What does he seem like?"

Simon hesitated when I asked him this. He said, "I don't really know your dad."

"From what you've seen of him."

"I only really know what you've told me. From what you've told me it sounds like he still loves your mum but he's feeling, like... hurt? And confused? Like she's throwing everything back in his face and he doesn't know what he's done to deserve it."

"He hasn't done anything to deserve it!" I cried. "He just doesn't understand!"

"Could be that's the key to it. Once he does—"

"They'll get back together again? You really think so?"

"Maybe if you help them," said Simon.

What he thought I could do, I really didn't know, but at least it gave me something to hold on to. Afterwards I thought what a lovely guy he was, and what a shame he was physically challenged. What Dad in his non pc way would call crippled, but that is such a hateful word. It was how I'd thought of Simon when I'd first seen him; but now that I'd got to know him, and especially now we'd both *bared our souls* – well, my eyes and his leg! – I just thought of him as Simon, who happened to walk with a limp.

It was still a shame, cos actually he was really quite attractive, I could really have gone for him. I mean, if I hadn't gone for Matt first. Anyone would have gone for Matt first! Like when me and Hattie were together, boys always went for me first. It was just a fact of life, I wasn't claiming any credit for it.

And then it occurred to me... maybe Simon would make a good partner for Hattie on Founder's Day? If she hadn't already got one, that is. I'd promised to look out for her, but what with my eyes swelling up and Mum dropping her bombshell, I'd forgotten all about it. Hattie herself hadn't mentioned it, so I assumed she was still partnerless. Not that you *had* to have a partner, but most everybody did. Poor old Hat! It would be horrible if she was the only person on her own. And it wouldn't really matter that Simon couldn't dance, cos Hattie isn't that much of a dancer. She wouldn't mind. They could sit and talk together. They'd get on really well!

I was so pleased to have solved the problem, I thought that I would tell Hattie the very next day, when I went back to school.

Matt rang that evening. He was all jokey, so I was all jokey too. He said, "My spy tells me you're fit to be seen again?"

I said, "Yup! I can go out without frightening people."

I wasn't really feeling jokey. Really I would have liked to ask him who he had planned on going to Founder's Day with, if not me. But I wasn't quite brave enough, so we just fooled around a bit and Matt said it was a pity he hadn't discovered sooner that I didn't look like a pickled walnut any more cos then we could have met up, maybe, at the weekend.

"Unfortunately it's too late, now, I've gone and arranged something else."

Still being all jokey I said, "I hope it's not anything too exciting!"

"How could it be exciting," said Matt, "if you're not there?"

Hopefully I said, "I *could* be there."

"I wish," said Matt.

He never did tell me what he was doing. He said we would speak again after the weekend and then rang off, leaving me feeling vaguely dissatisfied. That night I wrote in my diary for the first time in weeks.

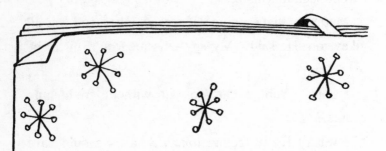

Matt called. Simon has told him I am back to normal and will be all right for Founder's Day. Next week! Matt said, "Talk about leaving things till the last minute." He said, "I was getting a bit worried, there. I didn't fancy going with a pickled walnut!" I guess I should be grateful that he has waited for me. A boy like Matt, he could have any girl he wanted.

I am quite looking forward to it, though somehow not as much as I

thought I would be. I don't know why.
I'm sure it will be fun when we get
there.

Tomorrow I am going back to
school. I am still a bit self-
conscious, even though Simon has
assured me I don't look pickled any
more, and I know he wouldn't lie, not
even to be kind. He is very
trustworthy. Thank heavens Hattie
is the only person who knows why I've
been away. I told her to tell everyone
I had the flu, otherwise they would
all be peering at me. I couldn't take
that!

Next morning I met up with Simon at the station and
we travelled in together. He said, "How are you
feeling?" I said, "Nervous!"

"No need," said Simon. "You look great!"

I thought again how nice he was, and what a
comfort. Just for a moment I almost wished I were
going to Founder's Day with him instead of with Matt,
but the moment passed. Matt might not be as nice and
he certainly wasn't as comforting, but he was utterly

and totally the most gorgeous boy I had ever been out with. Tanya's eyes, when she saw me with him, were going to jump right out of their sockets!

Hattie was waiting for us when we got off the train. She needn't have, cos I'd told her I was coming back to school and so there wouldn't be any homework for her to pick up, but she said she'd kind of got used to it.

"Anyway," she said, "as it's your first day back I thought you'd like some company."

I beamed at her, gratefully. There are times when Hattie can be just *so* thoughtful.

"You didn't tell anyone?" I said.

"Not a soul! Honest! Cross my heart and hope to die."

If Hattie said she hadn't told anyone, then she hadn't. She is always, absolutely, one hundred per cent truthful and she isn't a prattler. In other words, she is not one of those people that open their mouths and just let stuff pour out in a mindless stream. I hate people like that! Hattie said she hadn't told and I believed her. So how come Tanya knew??? She made a beeline straight for me, all oozing with sympathy and a kind of patronising gush.

"Scarlett, are you OK now? God, you poor thing, it must have been awful! I'd be absolutely petrified if anything like that happened to me. I'd think I was going to be scarred for life! Did you just wake up one morning and find it had happened?"

Someone said, "Find what had happened?"

"Her eyes," said Tanya. "They all swelled up!"

"*Really?*"

As brightly as I could I said, "Like footballs. I had to wear sunglasses or people would just have dropped dead on the spot."

Tanya said, "I would have dropped dead on the spot if I woke up and found my eyes had turned into footballs. It's the most horrific thing I've ever heard!"

"But why did it happen? What caused it? What was it?"

Now they were all clamouring at me, like a load of ghouls.

"Oh, I'm just a bit allergic," I said.

"You are so *brave*," said Tanya. "If that had been me… "

She threw up her arms and went, "*Aaaargh!*"

It didn't help that I suspected she was quite genuine. In other words, she wasn't deliberately trying to upset me. Tanya is quite maddeningly *nice*.

"Well, anyway," said Hattie, "it's all cleared up."

"Yes, thank goodness," said Tanya. "You wouldn't ever know, unless you peered *really* closely."

So then, of course, they all had to peer at me until I felt like some kind of exhibit in a freak show. I wailed at Hattie later.

"How did she find out?"

"I dunno," said Hattie. "I didn't tell her, I promise!"

"But who else knew?"

"No one – except Matt and Simon."

"They wouldn't have told her!"

"Simon wouldn't," said Hattie. "Matt might have done… maybe it was Matt?"

"But he doesn't even know her!"

"Well… he did meet her at the fundraiser. When she won the beauty contest? Which you would have won," said Hattie, "if you'd been there, and which is the only reason he actually came, cos he thought you *were* going to be there, only of course you weren't, so—"

"D'you mean he talked to her?" I said.

"Yes. Well! Yes," said Hattie.

"They didn't go off together, or anything?"

"No! I don't think so."

"Well, did they or didn't they?"

"I don't know!"

"You might have told me at the time," I said.

"How could I tell you when *I didn't know?* And anyway, what's to tell? He just went and, like, congratulated her, for goodness' sake! Oh, and I think they might have met up at a swimming gala." She tossed this bit out all casually, like it was of no significance whatsoever. "The interschools thing? A couple of weeks ago? I don't know for sure. It's just what someone said… that Tanya had met this gorgeous bloke. I mean, it might have been someone totally different. It probably wasn't Matt at all. I really don't know."

A fat lot of help *she* was. I tortured myself all evening. I completely forgot that I'd been going to offer Simon to Hattie; I forgot that she was still partnerless. All I could think of was Matt with Tanya…

Next morning I went marching up to Tanya at the start of school and asked her, straight out, "You weren't thinking of going to Founder's Day with Matt by any chance, were you?"

Well, huh! At least I had the

satisfaction of seeing her thrown into some kind of panic. She's very together, is Tanya; it takes a lot to rattle her. But she deserved it, is all I can say. Poaching someone else's property! Cos I knew at once she was guilty. I'd have known even if she hadn't gone bright red like a tomato.

"You mean Matt Stanton?" she said.

I said, "Yeah, I mean Matt Stanton."

"Oh! Well – no, not really. I mean… only if you weren't going to be OK in time." And she gave this silly little apologetic tinkle. "See, the boy I was going to go with can't make it, so I just thought… if you were going to have to back out—"

"You'd jump in in my place."

"No! It wasn't like that. Honestly, Scarlett! I was thinking of Matt, he was going to be so disappointed if you couldn't make it. He knows Founder's Day is a big thing and he's been just *so* looking forward to it."

I said, "Yeah, it would be really sad."

"Well, I think so," said Tanya.

She is such a truly *annoying* sort of person. Always so sweet and reasonable. Yuck!

"So who are you planning to go with now?" I said.

"Oh, I'll find someone. Don't worry about me," said Tanya.

Like she really thought I would? Pur-lease!

When I told Hattie about it, she said she didn't think it was fair to put all the blame on Tanya.

"What about Matt?"

"Well, but if she went and asked him," I said, "you couldn't expect him not to go… not if I wasn't able to."

"Why not?" said Hattie. "Why couldn't he come round and spend the evening with you, instead?"

"Oh, God," I said, "I wouldn't want him to do that! The state I was in."

But I knew that wasn't the real answer. The real answer was that Matt was not the sort of boy to spend quiet evenings in when he could be out enjoying himself – specially if he could have a girl like Tanya hanging on his arm.

I brooded silently to myself during afternoon school. I came to the conclusion that Matt was nothing but a status symbol. We would go to Founder's Day together and all the older people would look at us and go ooh and aah and say what a handsome couple we made, and the younger ones – well, the girls – would be consumed with envy; and it would all be very satisfying, on a kind of superficial level, and I would enjoy the attention, cos I do like attention, but it would be *absolutely hollow*. That was my conclusion. Hollow! I wasn't even sure that I wanted Matt to be my partner any more. I had this vision of telling him so. I sat at the back of Mr Dainty's geography class and let the vision unfold…

*I'm afraid I just don't want to go with you any more. I'm sorry, but that's the way it is.*

*Scarlett, my God, how can you do this to me? How can you be so cruel? I've been so looking forward to it!*

*Boo hoo. That is just so sad! But I'm sure you'll find someone else to ask you.*

*I don't want anyone else, I want you! You're the one I've always wanted. Scarlett, please! I'm begging you!*

Well, OK, so perhaps it wasn't very realistic, but at least it was fun and paid him back for even *thinking* of going to Founder's Day with someone else. In my vision, I graciously handed him over to Tanya, telling her she could have him and welcome.

"I'm going to ask someone far nicer!"

*Simon.* That was who I was going to ask!

I grew quite excited as I thought about it. I forgot – yet again – that I'd been going to offer him to Hattie. Perhaps I didn't exactly forget; perhaps I just preferred not to remember. It did make me feel a bit bad. Poor old Hat! On the other hand, I was sure I could find someone for her if I really put my mind to it, which I would – I would! – just as soon as I'd got my own problems sorted. Plus I couldn't help reflecting that it would be the hugest feather in Simon's cap if he were to go to Founder's Day as my partner. It would do wonders for his self-esteem!

I grabbed Hattie the minute school let out. "Hey! Guess what?"

"What?"

"I've decided... I'm not going to Founder's Day with Matt, after all."

"Oh?" She widened her eyes. "So who're you going with?"

"Simon!"

"*Simon?*"

Hattie's jaw did this comic clunking thing. I might have laughed if I hadn't been so fired up with my own mad enthusiasm.

"I know, I know! It sounds completely crazy, when he can't even dance. He'll probably get all silly and self-conscious and try to wriggle out of it, but I am not taking no for an answer! I'm going to call him tonight and ask him. Correction: I'm going to *tell* him. I'm going to *order* him. He's coming with me whether he likes it or not! Then everyone will be able to see that *the great Scarlett Maguire*—" I twizzled my fingers round the words as I said them, making quote marks in the air to show I was just joking. I didn't *really* think of myself as great "—everyone'll be able to see that it doesn't matter to me *in the least little bit* about his leg. It'll show him, as well, cos you know what he's like, he just gets *so* wound up about it. I mean, he pretends not to care, but you can tell that he does. It was like me and my eyes. I mean, I can sympathise cos I've, like, been there. I've hidden myself away. But I actually got him into the pool the other day! Did he tell you? I actually got him swimming! So—"

At this point in my burbling stream of words, something brought me to a full stop. It was Hattie's face. Her jaw had cranked itself back up into its normal position, but her face had been growing steadily pinker by the second,

so that it was now like a big setting sun, all blood red and throbbing.

"What's the matter?" I said.

Hattie swallowed.

"S-Simon—" she bleated.

"What about him?"

Now she was gulping, like a gold fish. "I've already—"

"What? You've already what?"

"I've already asked him!"

This time, it was my jaw going clunk. "You've asked him? To be… my partner?"

"*My* partner."

"*Your* partner?"

"Yes!" Hattie nodded; rather too vigorous and secretly pleased with herself for my liking.

"So what did he say?"

She beamed. "He said he'd love to!"

"I see." I just said it to give myself time to think. This was a real bombshell! "When, exactly, did you ask him?"

"Last night… I rang him."

And there was me, not even knowing she had Simon's number. Hattie can be *such* a dark horse.

"Scarlett, I'm sorry, I know I should have told you. I was going to, it's just—"

"Oh, don't worry, don't worry!" I said. "If he'd rather go with you, that's fine."

"Well, I'm sure he wouldn't *rather.*" She was blushing again, all bright fiery red. "I don't suppose anyone would *rather.* Not if they could go with you."

"You don't have to butter me up!" I said.

"I'm not, it's true, it'd be so much more *prestigious* for him if he went with you. I can see that!"

So maybe she should ring him again?

*Simon, it's wonderful, Scarlett's gone and junked Matt and wants you to go with her, instead!*

But she didn't offer. She said, "I wouldn't have asked him if I'd known you were going to. If only you'd told me before!"

I snapped, "I didn't know before."

"No. Well—" Hattie spread her hands. She looked at me, beseechingly. "What can I do?"

I certainly wasn't going to tell her; it had to come from her. If she were really thinking of Simon rather than herself—

She obviously wasn't. She was obviously being

175

*totally* self-centred. I suppose I couldn't really blame her, but still it was considerably annoying.

"You'll still come," she begged, "won't you?"

I said I couldn't make any promises. "To be honest, I'm kinda going off the idea."

"Oh, Scarlett, *please!*" said Hattie. "Don't make me feel guilty!"

Serve her right if she did. Fancy going and asking Simon off her own bat, without even bothering to tell me! I felt like pointing out that *I* was the one who was supposed to be finding a partner for her. I was working on it! I'd got someone in mind!

Only I hadn't, so I shut up.

I decided that after all I had better stick with Matt. At least he was a status symbol, and at least it meant Tanya wouldn't be able to get her thieving hands on him.

Next morning, on the way in to school, I told Simon how glad I was that he was going to partner Hattie. I meant it. I really did! I *was* glad. It would have been mean not to be, for Hattie's sake. I just had this feeling that if I'd only got in first...

"It's so lovely for Hattie," I said. "I'd promised to find someone for her, and it just went right out of my head!"

Simon said, "That's OK. It's only thanks to you that I'm going."

I said, "*Really?*" What had I done???

"That day you forced me into swimming?"

"Oh," I said, "yes!" And I gave a little laugh, to show that I was cool with it. "You made me show my face and I made you take your trousers off!"

"We made each other brave," said Simon. "If Hattie had asked me the day before I'd have said no, I don't go to dances. So it was entirely thanks to you."

Oh, dear! It was very hard to bear. But there are times you just have to put a brave face on things.

I wasn't very brave when Mum finally packed her bags and left. Mum wasn't too brave, either: anyone would have thought she didn't want to go. At the last minute we clung to each other and she kissed me,  and I swear she had tears in her eyes, though I couldn't be certain cos I'd got this kind of mist thing going on and couldn't see properly.

"Mum," I whispered, "do you have to go?"

"I think I do," she said. "I think I really need to…

just to give myself a bit of space. But Scarlett, I'm only half an hour away! We'll see each other all the time. Why don't you come over on Saturday evening, and I'll make us something special, just the two of us, and you can tell me all about the Dinner and Dance... what d'you say? Shall we make a date?"

I said that I would like that.

"So would I," said Mum. She hugged me to her, very hard. "It's time you and I got to know each other!"

Dad and I stood watching as Mum's car turned out of the drive.

"She'll be back," said Dad. "All this nonsense!"

I said, "Dad, I don't think it is nonsense. I think Mum does honestly need to work out where she's going."

To which Dad merely said, "Huh!" and went stomping off into the house. I did feel sorry for him, cos I knew he really couldn't work out why Mum was doing this terrible thing, but I also knew that that was part of the problem. Until Dad understood, Mum couldn't come home. I was only just beginning to understand myself; it was going to be a lot harder for Dad. Simon had been right; it was up to me to help him. I wasn't quite sure how, except I had this feeling that me and Dad needed to do a lot more serious talking in the future. It wouldn't be easy, cos Dad really doesn't like serious talking, but you have to fight for the things that matter to you. And having Mum and Dad back together again mattered to me more than anything else in the whole world.

I didn't write in my diary about Mum leaving. I didn't even write about Founder's Day. I'd been looking forward to it for so long, up and down and over-the-moon so many times, but then in the end it came and went without so much as a mention. In fact it was months before I really started writing again and then only tiny snippets. I don't quite know why; it's not like I was specially unhappy or specially busy or specially anything. I guess it had just served its purpose and I didn't feel the need of it any more.

Founder's Day was fun, just not quite the earth-shattering event I'd built it up to be. I went with Matt and I suppose I might as well admit that it gave me a buzz, knowing he was way the most gorgeous guy there and that everyone was looking at us.

Well, OK, not everyone, that's a bit of a stupid exaggeration. But certainly lots of people. It was what I'd always wanted and I couldn't help basking, just a little. I think *anyone* would bask, in that situation. It's only human nature!

Loads of photos were taken, including one of me and Matt that appeared in the local newspaper. Dad was so proud! He ordered lots of big glossy prints and sent copies to all of our relatives. He also had one framed and put on the wall. *In his office*, thankfully, where I didn't have to cringe and listen to Dad telling everyone that came in, "This is my daughter Scarlett and her young man." I mean, it was a nice photo, someone even said that me and Matt were like the latest Hollywood golden couple and ought to be on the cover of *Hello!* magazine (which sent Dad into ecstasies) but Matt isn't "my young man", he never really was, and I'm long past the stage of wanting to be told all the time how beautiful I am. There are more important things in life! Besides, it's really immature.

Tanya was at the Dinner and Dance, of course. She came with a boy that everyone knew was her cousin. I did gloat a tiny bit, cos we'd been, like, rivals for so

long, and anyway she deserved it. Trying to poach Matt! But somehow it didn't make me feel as blissfully triumphant as I'd have thought it would. Just a little victory roll and then it was gone.

The big thing was Hattie and Simon. They were so sweet! It was like they were made for each other. They didn't do much in the way of dancing, but every time I looked in their direction they had their heads close, engaged in these really deep discussions. Well, I'm guessing they were deep! Knowing Hattie – knowing Simon. You can just bet they weren't involved in the silly sort of mindless frivolity me and Matt were. It was Hattie's turn to be over-the-moon and I was genuinely pleased for her. She's my friend and I couldn't be jealous. She deserved to be happy!

The next day, which was a Saturday, Matt rang. He wanted us to meet up that evening. Even after the way he'd treated me, my heart still leapt. I was still flattered that he wanted me. But I'd made a promise and I wasn't going to break it. Not even for the most gorgeous thing on two legs.

"Matt, I'm really sorry," I said, "I can't! I'm having dinner with my mum."

"On a Saturday?" said Matt. "Saturdays are for going out!"

I said, "I am going out... I'm going over to my mum's place."

"Yeah?" I could almost *see* his lip curling. I just knew that he was sneering. He said, "That sounds like a bundle of laughs!"

"She's my mum," I said.

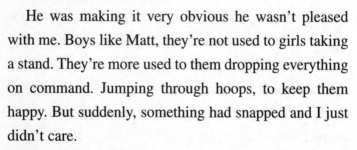

"OK, OK, so enjoy yourself. Have a ball!"

"Matt, I promised her," I said. "I can't not go!"

"Like I said, have a ball."

He was making it very obvious he wasn't pleased with me. Boys like Matt, they're not used to girls taking a stand. They're more used to them dropping everything on command. Jumping through hoops, to keep them happy. But suddenly, something had snapped and I just didn't care.

"Too bad if you don't like it," I said. "Why not try Tanya? She's desperate."

I am not going to write what Matt said in reply. It was just two words and one of them was rude. I was so angry that I said them straight back to him. Who did he think he was? God's gift to women?

Actually, I said that to him, as well, which made him say another two words, including the rude one, at which point I snarled, "Go boil yourself!" and slammed the phone down. I know it was really childish of me, but it was kind of satisfying. I bet I was the first girl who'd ever told the great Matt Stanton to go boil himself! Of course it meant that I was now boyfriendless, but I reckoned it was worth it, just for the pleasure of taking that conceited oaf down a peg or two. Tanya could have him and welcome. I wasn't standing my mum up for anyone!

Not even for Dad, who at the last minute came over all pathetic and said how could I desert him on his first weekend on his own?

"Let's go into town and have a meal! I'll take you to Rosetti's. Eh? How about that?"

"Dad, I can't," I said. "You know I've promised Mum!"

"That's all right, tell her you've had a change of plan… something's come up."

But I wouldn't; not even for Dad. I told him that maybe next week we could all go out together, him and Mum and me. I said, "You could take us somewhere extra special and show Mum that you still love her."

Dad said, "Of course I still love her! I'm not the one that's moved out."

"So let's arrange something," I said.

Dad muttered that Mum wouldn't want him tagging along, but he told me that I could go ahead and ask her, if I wanted. I knew he was feeling left out and sorry for himself, and that made me feel sorry for him, too. But I found that I wasn't cross with Mum any longer; I could sort of understand why she'd had to get away. I just wished Dad could! I wished I could talk to him. I needed to talk! I needed someone to tell me that I was doing the right thing, going off to see Mum and leaving Dad on his own.

In the end I did what I always do in moments of doubt: I rang Hattie. Hattie was still up in the air about

Simon, but she came back down to earth long enough to listen while I poured out my troubles.

"I promised Mum I'd go round, but Dad's so sad! I don't know if I ought to leave him. I don't know what to do! I don't want to let Mum down, but I don't want to desert Dad, either!"

Hattie, as usual, was calm and practical. She said, "You're not deserting your dad. You're just going round to see your mum! *Of course* you must go. If you don't mind my saying so, you've always been a bit of a daddy's girl. You've never given your mum a chance. It's time you got to know her better. I reckon that right at this moment your mum's the most important person in your life."

Hattie is such a comfort! Before speaking to her I'd been all muddled and anxious. Now I felt that I could see the way ahead a bit more clearly.

"Dear, darling Hattie," I said, "thank you *soo* much!"

"You're welcome," said Hattie.

I asked her what she was doing that evening, and going all bashful she said "Seeing Simon."

"Well, have an over-the-moon day!" I said.

"Yeah. Right," said Hattie. She obviously hadn't the faintest idea what I was talking about! "You, too."

I thought, not this evening; it was too soon for that. But for the first time in ages I did begin to believe that there *would* be over-the-moon days. I just had to work at it.

# Boys Beware

Everyone at school is just so envious of us!
Meg Hennessy couldn't believe that
we are truly independent.
"All on your own?" she kept saying.
"You're living completely on your own?"

Hi there. I'm Emily and my stepsister (and hugest best friend!) is
called Tash. We're into boys in a BIG WAY. Mum and Dad are
going away for a couple of months, leaving us in our own flat in
Aunty Jay's house, and we're going to have the most fun ever!

0-00-716138-7

# Sugar and Spice

Shay was totally drop-dead gorgeous.
Why would a person that looked like a model
want to sit next to *me* – an insignificant little
weed with a brace on her teeth? *And glasses.*

Geeky Ruth Spicer hates school. When super-cool Shayanne
Sugar comes along and – shock horror! – wants to be her
friend, things begin to look up. But Shay is hiding something.
Do best friends tell each other *everything*?

0-00-716137-9

Check out Jean Ure's website: www.jeanure.com
www.harpercollinschildrensbooks.co.uk

# Is Anybody There?

Last year, I did this really dumb thing.
I got into a car with somebody
I didn't know...

If mum had been an ordinary mum, she might have
got the truth out of me. But she's not an ordinary mum,
she's a clairvoyant, and she's always careful not to pry.
I didn't even tell Dee and Chloe, my two best friends.
And now I'm not the only one in trouble...

0-00-716136-0

Check out Jean Ure's website: www.jeanure.com
www.harpercollinschildrensbooks.co.uk

# Secret Meeting

"I'm your fairy godmother!" Annie sprang
off the bed and did a little twirl.
"I'm the one that makes your
dreams come true!"

Annie's arranged the coolest birthday present for her
best friend, Megan. She's surfed the Net, made the contacts,
and it's all sorted! Now all they need to do is to escape from
Annie's bossy older sister. Cos a secret meeting wouldn't
be the same if it wasn't, well, secret…

0-00-715620-0

Check out Jean Ure's website: www.jeanure.com
www.harpercollinschildrensbooks.co.uk

www.jeanure.com